MW00436220

Someone is Always Watching

"You know it's not *just* a toy," Tim said, gently. "That otter you keep on your desk has a camera in it."

"Everything has cameras in it," Lana sighed, the sheer weight of the fact suddenly pressing in on her, as inescapable as the midsummer sun's laser gaze.

"Exactly," Johnny said, squaring his torso with his hands on his hips as he squinted through the crowd. He had a determined look, which Lana suddenly envied.

Before she could speak, there was an abrupt knot of movement from the north end of the plaza—someone had flung something, a stone, and the NAPD officers surged into the breach of shocked gasps, the murmuring roar of movement. People in black jackets were immediately in her periphery, holding signs, pressing forward, a crowd swell that suddenly flung her aside. Johnny's look of determination was the last thing she saw before the forward rush of superheated bodies swept him away from her view.

"End privacy abuses!" a man's voice screamed, startlingly near Lana, as more bodies thundered past. Toward the north end of the plaza she saw the edge of the transplas barrier peeled away as if it were paper, scattering the frightened NBN staffers. Panic throbbed through the plaza. Lana felt suspended in that moment, when any more hesitation would bring the real and imminent risk of being trampled.

For thatbear, SpectralIMP, and especially Quinns.

Cover illustration by Darren Tan.

Color insert artwork by Aurore Folny, Imaginary FS Pte Ltd,
Adam Schumpert, and Matt Zeilinger.

ISBN: 978-1-63344-250-4

Printed in the United States of America.

Fantasy Flight Games
1995 West County Road B2
Roseville, MN 55113
USA

Find out more about Fantasy Flight Games
and our many exciting worlds at

www.FantasyFlightGames.com

An

Novella

Monitor

by Leigh Alexander

Fantasy Flight Games

CHAPTER 1

It wasn't that Lana Rael did not know she was always being watched. Even when she could not see the machinelike eyes that nested insidiously inside almost everything she touched, she could feel them watching, and it made the hair stand up on her arms like a chill. To live in New Angeles was to know that feeling intimately, like breathing. And, like breathing, it was easy to forget about, to stop noticing. Until there was some kind of problem.

Summer in New Angeles was always an assault on the senses. The sun was much too bright, filtering with laser cruelty through the heavy atmosphere, drawing the city's often incoherent shapes in brutal lines: here, the ruthless glitter of chrome and glass; there, pockets of superheated air flecked with urban dust, debris flicking along the crowded streets in step with the wilting crowd that pulsed and ambled on its bleak Sunday strolls.

Streets with noisome shopfronts swelled toward Plaza Centrale like the spokes on a wheel. Tendrils of vitality and human life seemed to surge up from the undercity, grasping at the edges of the plaza, jittering toward the shopping and transit hub in crooked lines. It was precariously jammed here, the clean glitter of the arcologies suspended in the distance, the darkly sloping underpasses plummeting into the riotous slums that lay only a few miles below, flickering shadows out of view. Lana's work shirt, still pinned with its MegaBuy-branded name tag, was damp in her carry bag, the hated thing crumpled away for a brief respite. She would have to put it on again tomorrow.

"At least we won't have another Sunday shift for a few weeks." His face glistening, Johnny threw a morose glance over his shoulder at Lana. Behind her, Tim kept pace, his pale skin already reddening in the late afternoon. The closer they drew to the center of the massive plaza, a silvereen heat shimmer that spread out as far as the eye could see, the more virt displays proliferated—flickering but vivid banners blinked advertisements into the superheated air. Outside El Puma, the friends' regular after-work haunt, a holo of a woman waved both hands at them as if welcoming a friend, the phrase *Come In and Cool Off* sketching itself across her apron. Lana averted her gaze, weaving aside as if it might actually touch her.

"Do you guys want to stop for a bit?" Tim looked hopeful. The familiar, often sparsely attended interior of the dark restaurant did look cool, spotted with a colorful spectrum of virts singing the day's jingles, scrolling the day's information. The same ads and news bulletins could be seen in almost every shopfront they passed, all of them gilded with the instantly recognizable sigil of NBN, the megacorp that governed the Network. You could squint down the crowded row of shoebox businesses and pick the logo out again and again, the glittering emblems like spider eyes, like shiny, friendly buttons.

"The demonstration is supposed to be starting soon," Johnny said, seeming to make an executive decision with a single shake of his head, and he pushed forward through the thickening crowd that gathered ahead of them, the noise of merry music, and the wash of vivid light. A yellow balloon sailed in a haphazard pattern overhead.

Lana met Tim's gaze with silent empathy. Her mouth, too, felt suddenly dry as they passed El Puma. She placed her hand on her friend's warm shoulder. "We should stick to the plan," she said gently. "Then let's go for drinks afterward."

The fountain at the center of this particular L-square had been shut off, choked with streamers and bunting. It looked like it had all been done by children, and maybe it had. Families were everywhere, crowding close to the barricades that surrounded a temporary stage garishly emblazoned with NBN branding. A gigantic, arching logo projection declared that they had reached the site of the *SUNSHINE JUNCTION SUMMER OUTDOOR FAMILY FUN DAY PLAY AND CONCERT.*

It certainly didn't look like a protest, at least not yet. The holographic animal friends from the *Sunshine Junction* "edutainment universe" were moving, flickering with surreal slowness on the big stage at the plaza's opposite end. Officers of the New Angeles Police Department stood at the fringes of the crowd, and farther back, among temporary shelters built out of transplas, NBN staff supervised and operated the show. The transparent barriers, lathed in heat shimmer, formed a nearly invisible wall between the company's workers and the attendees. Children shrieked at the barricade's edges, jostling to "meet" the animals, who were singing a song about how you should tell your neighbors not to litter, even though you might want to avoid conflict.

It was always the same setup: Problem-Solvin' Puppy, Diversity Otter, Empathy Cat, and Friendship Rabbit circled the constantly awkward Doofus Dinosaurus, whose antisocial behavior was regular cause for musical lectures on how to be a better community member. It was always treacly, but not particularly offensive, Lana thought.

"Training kids to be snitches from childhood," Johnny said pointedly, nodding at the display. Then he added, authoritatively, "The boards said the protest would happen. It's gonna be happening here."

Lana had met Johnny at university, when they'd been involved in the same activist groups: a pro–environmental education campaign group, a study group about the ethics of archived consciousness, and the Free Minds Club, a debate team on surveillance and corp access to consumer behavior. The villain then had been NBN, the great trawling data-miner that could supposedly see you anywhere, owned data on your habits and movements, and used that data to target you aggressively through all of its Network programming and services.

Privately, Lana felt that protesting a children's Netcast might not be the best use of their time. Ever since she and Johnny had started working together at MegaBuy, doing consumer services and fulfillment—that was where they'd met Tim—their free time had been at a premium. Johnny was always talking about getting involved in the "underground," making hacker contacts and joining the resistance. He was full of wild theories: *Sunshine Junction* was a ploy to deter antisocial behavior through consumer brainwashing, their shift lead at MegaBuy was secretly a freedom fighter, things like that.

"*You might be afraid you'll ruin their mood, but leavin' that trash was just plain rude,*" Lana found herself murmuring along with the display as the performance continued.

Johnny chortled so audibly that a father nearby, holding a rowdy child's hand, turned to look. The child was wearing an animal mask, and near him, a passel of teen girls were eagerly sporting *Sunshine Junction* PAD straps. Even Tim laughed under his breath. "Lana knows all the *Sunshine Junction* songs," Johnny teased her. "Lana doesn't care about the protest, she just wants a new *Sunshine Junction* toy."

"Hey," she replied, feeling herself redden a little. She'd felt a strange, empathetic pang when Johnny had thrown her *Sunshine Junction* desk mascot away, and had found herself rescuing it, sheepish but unyielding. "I very much care about the protest, but sometimes a toy is just a toy. I mean, I know it's, like, capitalist merchandising of—"

"You know it's not *just* a toy," Tim said, gently. "That otter you keep on your desk has a camera in it."

"Everything has cameras in it," Lana sighed, the sheer weight of the fact suddenly pressing in on her, as inescapable as the midsummer sun's laser gaze.

"Exactly," Johnny said, squaring his torso with his hands on his hips as he squinted through the crowd. He had a determined look, which Lana suddenly envied.

Before she could speak, there was an abrupt knot of movement from the north end of the plaza—someone had flung something, a stone, and the NAPD officers surged into the breach of shocked gasps, the murmuring roar of movement. People in black jackets were immediately in her periphery, holding signs, pressing forward, a crowd swell that suddenly flung her aside. Johnny's look of determination was the last thing she saw before the forward rush of superheated bodies swept him away from her view.

"End privacy abuses!" a man's voice screamed, startlingly near Lana, as more bodies thundered past. Toward the north end of the plaza she saw the edge of the transplas barrier peeled away as if it were paper, scattering the frightened NBN staffers. Panic throbbed through the plaza. Lana felt suspended in that moment, when any more hesitation would bring the real and imminent risk of being trampled. A woman with a mohawk shouldered her almost off her feet, and from elsewhere a fist or elbow struck Lana's ribs, briefly winding her.

She could try to escape, or she could run forward. Lana ran forward. She thought she saw Johnny's hair like a flag whipping downstream, flashing and then gone again, and then her body seemed to be moving slowly as if through water, thudding roughly up against the transplas shelter, or what was left of it. The stampeding crowd pinned her against the hard surface, and a swinging limb narrowly missed her temple, yanking one of her earrings along with her short hair. It felt like something tore.

I'm going to die protesting a children's edutainment universe, Lana thought dully. It felt like an eternity before her body hit the street.

At the last minute, knees and palms screaming, Lana pawed desperately into a little space between the broken barricade and the pavement, where the barricade walls would shelter her. She saw boots and uniformed trousers: the NAPD officers shuttling the executives away to safety. Debris hit her makeshift shelter as she heard the grind and shriek of the protesters tearing apart the projection equipment.

Something small and shiny caught her eye, lying just a few feet away. It was a brand-new PAD. It must have belonged to one of the staff, she realized, a shivering impulse she could not identify twinging haphazardly through her.

Unthinking, Lana reached for the device. Her fingers brushed asphalt, narrowly avoiding a tramping boot that inadvertently kicked the PAD, like a little puck, a few more inches out of reach. Her ribs aching, she strained her arm from behind the transplas, aware of the fragility of her grasping fingers, which just barely managed to close on the device and pull it to her, at last shoving it inside her carry bag underneath her MegaBuy work shirt.

Lana hid behind the transplas, curled in on herself. She could hear the unsettling howls of the crowd now from all around, but she could no longer make out the protesters' deep-throated, rhythmic antisurveillance chants. Equally as loud, the stage show continued, ghostlike neon colors flickering and looming on the stage, grinning animal friends presiding over the riot, singing their tinny, friendly neighborhood tune.

If she could just hide here until the police dispersed the crowd, Lana told herself calmly, repeatedly, she would survive.

And if she survived, she would never do this kind of thing again. Not like this. There had to be a better way. She would have to find it.

CHAPTER 2

The MegaBuy call center was a massive farm of eggshell-colored pods and out-of-date terminals, projections in dated hues washing out the faces of the reps on each line. The dim room pulsed with voices, usually reciting variations on the same script as they patched customers through the designated Conflict Resolution Tree. The reps worked under the constant scrutiny of their own vid units, every detail captured and analyzed. Every week came the all-important results of a new customer satisfaction survey, and adjustments were mandated: reps smiled too much this week, not enough the next. Lana had participated in a week-long program of customer body language training when she'd joined the team. Everything, down to the suggestion made by the movement of one shoulder versus both, could be optimized.

The loathsome surveys, though, were still something of a last bastion: the staff all knew they could easily be replaced by AI if it weren't for the fact the surveys always indicated a preference for a human face on the other side of the vid display.

Productivity research software installed on all their workstations had also revealed that reps performed better when they knew they were on camera.

Lana had been working at the call center for close to two months now—long enough to learn not to drop the calls or patch them through the Conflict Resolution Trees incorrectly, and long enough to start feeling trapped. Every day the alarm on her personal wrist PAD woke her in the dark of the morning; first thing, she always checked her messages. She had sent what felt like hundreds of applications to administration jobs at nonprofits, and every day there was nothing. Nothing except for a shower, the hated Mega-Buy work shirt and tie, and the dusty commute along transit lines, slowly heating with the sunrise as if she were leftover food.

Reps were each permitted one personal item at their designated pod. Lana's Diversity Otter toy stood beside her display, warm gray and round-bellied, wearing its blue goggles. When she looked directly at it for more than fifteen seconds, it would greet her: "Howdy, neighbor! Hope you're having a neighborly day!" She liked its sweet face and sweet voice, a little guiltily. It was only a toy. It wasn't Diversity Otter's fault that it was made by an evil corporation.

"Thank you for vidding MegaBuy; how can I help you?" It had been a long day, and Lana was desperate to reach the end of her queue. Probably they didn't see her as a person, she knew. She hated her own blanched face reflected back at her in the corner of the vid, washed in the acid orange of the display. Self-consciously, she tucked her dark hair behind her ears—it was not quite long enough to stick there yet and wisps came loose almost instantly, an ongoing payment for the impulsive decision to buzz it all off in junior year. She had been protesting oppressive beauty standards.

She felt she looked kind of like a teenager without her ear piercings, but policy forbade earrings.

Lana's customer service pod was directly beside Tim's, and Johnny sat behind her. Having friends around made her shifts at the call center marginally more bearable. Although Tim was quiet, he was kind, a bear of a boy who went by "Tiny Tim" on the Net boards and who always thought to bring canned coffee for all three of them. Johnny, though he often talked too much, was always funny, at least.

"I'm thinking of changing my handle again," he said as soon as she finished her call. "Calling myself 'Lucifer' only works if you know my name is John Milton, and if you know my name, what's the point?"

"Right," Lana said, half-listening.

"Devils are played, anyway. Right, Tim? Don't you think devils are played?"

"He's on a call," Lana said. Tim often spoke softly enough that it was hard to tell when he had a customer and when he was just sitting. "You could be 'Satan' instead," she added. She didn't know much about *Paradise Lost*—some old paperbook—only that Johnny was excited to share a name with the author.

"Even then, my avatar looks really generic: just, like, a devil with horns," he said, flipping his pen into the air deftly and palming it out of the air again. "It's stupid. I don't like it. I want to, like, lambaste wealth and corruption. Can you think of a name that lambastes wealth and corruption?"

"Lambastes," said Lana. She wasn't sure he was pronouncing it right.

"Tim, can you think of anything that lambastes wealth and corruption?" Johnny addressed their friend, who had disconnected from his call and turned around slowly in his chair.

"You're changing your avatar *again*?" Tim asked mildly, faintly pursing his lips.

But Johnny was already looking elsewhere. The shift lead, the much whispered-about shift lead, was coming their way, already wriggling out of her uniform tie with the sort of fervor one reserves for nooses. Out of everyone on Lana's line, the shift lead looked the least like a customer service rep—although she called herself "Carol," she did so with the sort of sneer that suggested it wasn't her actual name.

The supervisors were always writing her up. Her hair, cropped and half-shaved and streaked with color and tiny braids, wasn't policy. Her lip rings weren't policy. Carol wore her earrings on the service line and still never got fired, Lana noticed resentfully.

"Are you lusers still sitting here? Shift's over," she said, frowning down on them. "Get the hell outta here."

"We were just…" Johnny stood up awkwardly, jostling his squeaky office chair, grinning his whitest smile at her. "Lana and Tim and me, we were going to have drinks after work, like, an underground meeting thing, if you—"

"Hell nah," she sang back almost brightly, making something like a salute as she walked away.

"An 'underground meeting'?" Tim frowned at Johnny. It was a sympathetic look.

"One of these days she's gonna say yes," Johnny said, with certainty. "And then we'll get let in on all her secrets. I just know she's, like, *someone*. Her PAD is tricked out. Why would some random MegaBuy rep have such a sweet PAD?"

"I'll bet she's just in a band," Lana said, feeling her mouth twist as she switched off her display. Tim shouldered his omnipresent messenger bag, and Johnny zipped his dark-green hoodie directly over the uniform shirt. Lana shrugged into her jacket a little bit gingerly, something that felt like a bruise still singing along her ribs from the weekend at the *Sunshine Junction* show.

She still had the stolen PAD. It sat like a stone in her jacket pocket, heavy as a guilty secret.

"We'll find out when we're a bigger deal," said Johnny, and they pressed outside into the humid night. The sun was always hanging low in the sky by the time they got out of work, spilling blood-red tendrils into the segment of the city plunged into mute shadow by the towering arcologies. The massive service center occupied an entire L-square on the plaza level, and the nearest Metro stations were a bleak fifteen-minute walk through ruddy, littered roads that led well below the plaza and among scrappy neighborhoods that hung on for dear life there, inconsistently lit by lights that blinked and spat from the stress on the city grid in summer.

Lana and the boys made their usual walk below the plaza's rim, pressing into the usual knot of nightlife: overcrowded food stalls shoved side by side against one another like stacks of damp newspaper, underground clubs that were just beginning to stir, belching dissonant noise and dyed-hair punks up from below, dregs gathering on broken staircases.

Johnny walked ahead. He had an elegant stride, elbows akimbo, long skinny legs jittering out a rhythm that, for better or for worse, Lana had been following for the past several weeks. She hadn't really been a drinker in school, but since then she hadn't found any better way to create a clean snap in the day between the gray routine of MegaBuy and her quiet nights at home alone with her Netcasts.

El Puma was nothing special; it was just the biggest bar between here and public transport. With its sad, cloudy tropical fish aquarium and dusty electric paintings, it was never so crowded they had to wait to be served or had to yell to hear one another talk, which was good enough for Lana—though Johnny's bouncing knee and fevered two-beer future-planning frequently served to suggest to her that there *had* to be better places out there, glorious places they were simply missing out on. Out there, to hear him tell it, were the kinds of places they all *belonged*, with velveteen banquettes and beautiful girls and famous dissidents.

As usual, there were just a few crusty-looking regulars at the bar, likely nursing pints since the afternoon, and the hostess greeted them at the door as if she'd been waiting. She was blank-faced and ageless, an uncomfortable seam running along the junction of her jaw and neck, her eyes lamp-like and uncanny.

"Hi," Lana said to the hostess, who did not respond.

"Isn't it a little weird you always talk to that old bioroid?" Johnny said as the three took their usual corner table. Its glass top had been freshly wiped down, but remained muddy with the kind of streaks that only come up with genuine care.

Lana felt the same kind of lonesome pang she'd felt when he and Tim suggested she should get rid of her otter toy. But Johnny was already on his way to order at the bar, already onto the next idea.

"Carol kind of smiled at me today," Johnny insisted as he and Tim carried three canned drinks to the table.

"I thought her name was Susan," Tim said, sidling glacially around the table to sit down.

"I've got yours today, Tim," said Lana. Tim gave her a bashful nod. He worked two MegaBuy shifts—from what Lana could gather, though he hardly shared much, Tim's mother was sick, and his sister was still in school, and he gave them part of his wages. Usually she and Johnny bought their own lunches and gave Tim the abysmal canned lunches that MegaBuy provided to day and evening workers.

Blood-colored streetlight and the last wan strains of day were still filtering through the dusty windows, and a news projection hung over the bar, where the regulars fanned themselves in languid rhythms. The sound was just a low buzz, but Lana idly read the news tickers: *Anarchists launch terror attack at children's outdoor fun day,* and *Three injured as itinerant protesters damage NBN property.*

"Notice," Johnny said floridly, jabbing a long, smooth thumb in the direction of the virt. "NBN controls the news, and NBN controls *Sunshine Junction*, so it's not like they're going to talk about the *truth* of what happened on the weekend. It was oppression. It was definitely oppression."

On the projection, the looming face of Empathy Cat appeared as part of an advertisement for smart home cooling: "*We'd all like to live in Sunshine Junction, but networked climate control products are the next best thing! Be a cool cat!*" In the advert, the animals showed a sweating Doofus Dinosaurus how to receive a low-cost upgrade by filling out a comprehensive renter's survey.

"This is what I'm talking about," said Johnny, pointing more insistently. "It's not just a cartoon for NBN to get merchandising money from: it's, like, this whole *mind control* thing. You see what I mean, Lana? You get that it's not just about the toys and the...the multimedia universe, right?"

Lana saw what Johnny meant, and had for some time. But her mellow agreement never seemed to cool the fires of his anger. She leaned forward. In body language training, she had learned that leaning forward meant the customer was interested and attentive.

"Maybe we should do a public information campaign, like some kind of daily Netcast," she said hopefully. "Tim, maybe one of your connections could set something that up."

"No," said Johnny, a little loudly. "No."

"It's been tried a bunch," Tim said, a faintly apologetic look on his face. "People with more advanced software than ours have tried, and the best of those Netcasts stay up half a day at most."

"Three college grads taking on NBN in an ordinary *information war* just isn't going to work, Lana," Johnny said, propping his elbows on the table and tenting his fingers in a put-upon way. "We're going to need to make a bigger bang. Like, save up our money, get skull ports, really jack in and *tear shit up.*"

"Saving that much would take four and a half years each," Tim said. It wasn't the first time he'd had to remind Johnny.

"Jack in and, like, swing my fist right into that Doofus Dinosaurus's face," Johnny went on.

"Dinosaurus is a victim too," Lana said, and heard a nervous giggle escape her own lips unexpectedly.

"It's not fragging funny, Lana," Johnny said, palm to forehead. "It's like I'm the only one here who cares about an uprising. Wait, *uprising*. Like, what if I called myself 'Icarus'? Because I'm rising from the flames?"

"That's a phoenix," Tim said, mouth partially hidden behind his drink. He was probably trying not to laugh, too. "Icarus is the one who—"

"John 'Icarus' Milton," Johnny tried on.

Gentle pink and blue tones from a nearby holo washed across the smeared glass tabletop. It was the *Sunshine Junction Dinner Hour*, the familiar animal characters paw in paw for their greeting tune, a bright-yellow sun stamped with the NBN logo looming over their heads.

"The thing is," Johnny said—and then again, as Lana had let her attention wander distractedly to the program. "The thing is, people know they're giving NBN their information. They just don't really get what NBN does with it. They think it's just—how does the song go?"

"*Keeping you safe at play and labor, sharing info makes good neighbors,*" Lana said, faintly embarrassed. The characters moved like lurid ghosts on the program in the background. "*Products and services just for you; come on, kids, you know what to do.*"

Johnny and Tim stared.

"I just have a good memory," Lana said, feeling herself redden.

"I mean, you know," said Johnny, "you *know* it's more sinister than that. You did all the slogans for Free Minds Club at school, Lana! This *Sunshine Junction* shit is raising a generation to be, like, totally comfortable with the surveillance state! It's like how you put medicine in applesauce to get a kid to eat it."

"I think...that's dogs," Tim interjected apologetically.

"Dogs don't eat applesauce," Johnny sighed. "It's bad for them. Now listen. If we had some kind of proof, right, something definitive *stolen* from the inside, we could do something. Tim, you know people with muscle, right? Don't you have connections?"

Tim shifted a little, something like a nod.

"We could get some data and sell it, even," Johnny said. "Tim, you could sell it and pay all your mom's medical bills."

"Maybe," he said. "Mostly I just want to do something that... she can be proud of."

Johnny ignored this. "Lana, come on, you can't make a difference in the world just by drawing fragging *posters* and writing slogans."

The customer service manual had taught Lana that the angle of Johnny's shoulders meant a fragile temper, and that the representative should use a gentle tone.

"What do you think we're supposed to do?" she snapped.

Out of the corner of her eye, Lana saw her wrist device signaling a new message. It was from her dad, who only ever left messages when it was something to do with money. Her rent was about due, and he'd been threatening to stop helping. Her guts knotted despite themselves, and she took a long sip of her beer.

"I, ah," she heard herself say, ghostlike, but Johnny was speaking over her.

"Get something physical off them. Just one piece of NBN corporate machinery. It would probably have, like, approved credentials, at least, something we could use to expose the data mining operations. Right, Tim?"

"It might, if we had a PAD or something."

The tiny pill of yellow light, its blinking alert insisting *DAD*, was suddenly irksome to Lana, and she pulled the mesh sleeve of her summer shirt over the wrist device. "Um, I—you guys?"

They turned to her. Johnny looked as if he were already going to dismiss her idea, but Lana dug in her handbag and produced the wedge-shaped PAD, the one she'd filched from the protest. It was scratched, but not broken.

"I picked this up on Sunday," she said softly.

"Holy," Johnny said, his attention snapping to her almost uncomfortably. His eyes were suddenly saucer-like, hungry spaces opening up. "Put that away," he added, hissing.

"Wow," said Tim, and even he was looking at Lana with something like awe. She felt her cheeks grow hot, and she hid the PAD before anyone else saw it.

"Why didn't you tell us?" Johnny asked, scratching his head, fidgeting, his sharp knee bobbing under the bar table. "When were you going to?"

"I just..." *forgot*, she was going to say, except it would be mostly a lie. "I was going to surprise you guys," she said, and let a small smile cross her face. "I pulled it off one of the executives during all the craziness." *Let's see Carol or Susan or whoever from work steal corporate hardware,* Lana thought.

"Tim," said Johnny, "what do you think we could get with that?"

"Maybe authenticated user data," he demurred, rubbing his chin. "There could be a pattern of permission that an NBN server would recognize."

"Like a key," Johnny said. "A key to a *Sunshine Junction* server. And we could get in and rip it up."

"Well, you'd need to have brain-nets or something for that."

"Expensive," said Johnny, knuckling his eye sockets.

Lana resolved she would listen to her Dad's message in the morning. "Tim, can you find us some brain-nets? Like, to borrow? Or secondhand?"

"I could ask around," he said, and then he noticed both of them were looking at him hopefully. "I mean, I think so."

"This is it," said Johnny. He took a big swig of his beer and proclaimed, "This is like the beginning of, like, a heist threedee."

Then Johnny raised his glass, and Tim and Lana did too. *Clink.* "This is gonna be big," he said.

Chapter 3

The biometric readout, the retinal scan. Several delicate, radiant lines resolved into a projection of a thin, pale face, dark curls pulled back severely. Although NBN employees were told not to smile for their employee file photos, the slightest hint of one pulled at the corners of the mouth nonetheless.

Her name etched itself beneath the image, an affirmation of her own identity, a ritual she performed every day when she came to work. *Rebekka Gleeson, Executive Programming Lead, Global Adaptive Entertainment Netcasting Solutions. Clearance level 98.* A soft chime, and the transparent security gate whispered gently apart for her to pass.

Bex Gleeson had a stride so long she tailored her pants for it. Sleeves, too, sitting like cobweb just at the spot where her fine wrists ended and her long-fingered hands began. High-collared suit jacket, just veiling the blue-white bouquet of her collarbones. The synthetic fiber hallway muffled, ever so gently, the gunfire of her sharp heels. She was precisely on time for her program status check-in. She would not lose one half-second between here and the planning room.

Bex had been expecting Victoria Jenkins at the other side of the table, but the big boss was absent today. Instead it was Jackson Howard in her place, vivid in one of his signature suits. They kept him youthful, he was known to assert—the saturated colors, like his office full of *Sunshine Junction* character models, were a constant temple to the work of engaging and entertaining all the world's children with exciting interactive brand solutions.

Bex felt her stomach turn. She absolutely couldn't stand him.

"Hi, my friend," Howard began warmly, tenting his fingers on the projection table as Bex sat down across from him. His grin was like the taste of synthetic sugar. Why Howard? Why today?

"I'll be leading the status meetings with each programming vertical for today, I'm afraid," he said, and laughed, even though nothing was funny. "I've been asked to do a little check-in with you, to talk about how some of your Net packages are performing this season," he continued. "You know the organization has always appreciated your disruptive concepting and the innovations you've devised across our exhaustive database of real-time community-oriented livefeeds."

"Thank you," Bex replied automatically. She set her PAD on the glass top, prepared to offer her presentation: *Student Debtors in Love* had performed above expectations, especially within the coveted eighteen- to twenty-four year-old male demographic, and *It Happened to Us: Backstage Beauty Pageant Brawls* had seen moderate year-over-year audience growth, impressive given saturation in the low-end celebrity surveillance market.

"Oh, that isn't necessary," Howard said, laughing, white-toothed, at volume. "I've personally reviewed your midseason numbers, and I know you are performing to expectations. The thing is, Bex, we're facing some additional viewership challenges this season, and while NBN knows that *to expectations* is all we've ever really demanded of our talent, we all need to buckle in for a little bit of a bumpy quarter. There are several constraints to our normative strategy, and we strive, of course, to take advantage of emerging markets and ongoing climate challenges—"

"Right," Bex said, feeling impatience flicker through her pin-straight frame. Why couldn't Chief Executive Jenkins handle this meeting? Why did it have to be Jackson Howard?

"Of course, I don't need to tell you that it's always a little more difficult to capture viewership in the summer months, especially among the working population, and these annual declines have been compounded year over year for the past three years," Howard replied. Though he had a tone of genuine concern, as if this data were of deeply personal import to him, the Old-Hollywood crag of his waxen smile never smoothed. "And while everyone at NBN of course just wants to focus on engaging new entertainment content for all of our loyal users, we can't ignore the unfortunate impact of civil unrest on our business model. My own program has been targeted—"

"You mean that *Sunshine Junction* incident," Bex said. "Did—"

"*Incident* is putting it lightly, my friend," Howard replied ruefully, looking at the ceiling. "I know you feel a strong sense of ownership over your work, and I have no intention to challenge that, of course, merely to ask for your empathy. Empathy is one of the cornerstones of community."

"Some drifters threw rocks at your holos, sir," she replied evenly. "I wouldn't say the company needs to—"

"Even small injuries can feel harmful." Howard made a boyish, wounded face, as if Bex herself had thrown a rock at him. With infuriating softness, he continued: "The *Sunshine Junction* Friends are more than an entertainment property—they are an enrichment initiative, remember. A community-building tool. It's our frontline strategy to build relationships with the next generation so that we can continue to watch over our users with more closeness, serving them more custom content than ever before."

Privately Bex loathed *Sunshine Junction*, its canned jingles and plastic smiles, the way that technicolor toys had started sprouting like mushrooms all across the offices over the past several years. She hadn't expected the "friends and neighbors" and "diversity and empathy" stuff to be as marketable as it had been. Beside it, she privately knew her own work ran the risk of seeming tawdry, and it worried her.

"My own programs continue to focus on the intimate stories of New Angelinos," Bex asserted. "I think we need a balance in our programming, between the…community building and the kind of raw, honest portraiture of my work. It's by exposing the things people keep hidden that—"

Howard laughed. *Why did he laugh so much, it was weird—*

"Of course, my friend," Howard began. "Your programs are excellent. Your work is always excellent, and you will always have a place here within NBN. But I must impress on you how urgent it is we begin to shift all hands toward our future-proof initiatives for the time being, especially our top-tier talent, which of course includes yourself. What we're seeing from the data is that people are hoping for a warm, positive experience when they tune in. They want the sense that they are *cared for* by media, and it's our job to provide content that gives people the opportunity to feel good about themselves, like they are being looked out for and are in turn looking out for one another."

"You want *me* to work on *Sunshine Junction*? Mr. Howard, that's not what I—"

"Not at all, friend," Howard said, cranking back his oddly smooth jaw for another open-mouthed, thunderous mannequin chortle. "We are not reassigning you just yet. To put it more clearly, I need you to replace one of your ordinary programs with a truly exciting new innovation that will enhance our existing verticals and become an essential pillar of our community-building efforts. These things you call *incidents* are a threat to the viability of all of our future programming initiatives, and we must rise to the challenge of discouraging and conquering this sort of customer dissatisfaction."

"How do you think I should—"

"Now Bex, my friend, I wouldn't dream of telling you how to do your distinct and utterly special work!" Howard showed all of his teeth, rubbing his palms together briskly. "I've had the operations team put aside several weeks' worth of *incident* footage files for you to review. To work your magic on, so to speak. I'm sure you can come up with something."

Incident footage? Did he think her shows about conflict and passion and humankind at its ugliest were the same thing as surveillance of people throwing rocks at cartoons? Bex felt the fury spreading white-hot across the fine bones of her chest, yanking on some hard wire inside her, but merely nodded.

Howard gave another plasticine grin, hinged-jaw laugh drifting into the air like warm toxin. "I look forward to seeing what you come up with for the remainder of the season. Please submit it to the board within the next forty-eight hours. That's all for now—and remember this season's Programming Department mission statement: 'Everyone is looking for a reason to feel like a hero in their own neighborhood.' I think people are fundamentally good, don't you, friend?"

Friend. Everything was "friend" this and "community building" that, Bex thought darkly, stung, making long, clipped strides back to her own office suite. When had that happened? Five years ago her department's mission statement was "What do you have to hide?", and you were supposed to think about how remapping social values about privacy would lead to high-impact universal human truths. Bex had built *Miranda Rhapsody: Pieces of My Soul* almost entirely on her own, on less than half the usual budget, using hundreds of thousands of hours of public data and surveillance. The other leads had worried that it was too raw, thinking that it would harm the singer. But the result was just the opposite: people loved the illicit, the too-intimate, the sense that they were looking at all the things the bubblegum superstar would rather you didn't. *Pieces of My Soul* became one of the company's top-selling threedees, and then all kinds of celebrities wanted voyeuristic portraits of themselves after the same fashion. They paid to commission them. And people ate those up, too, and then they wanted "uncut and intimate" looks at fights and diseases and all kinds of things, the uglier the better.

That was when Bex had started working through the nights alone, insisting on doing everything herself. She found she concentrated better when she took stims, and she didn't want anyone else seeing her like that, white-knuckled and glassy, especially as her tolerance increased and she needed more of them. And really, no one else understood what it took. It was too hard to describe. She imagined herself like some kind of divine insect, sprawling claw-like over the world with a thousand all-knowing eyes. Underneath her, human beings clamored, small and awful, constantly wishing to peep inside one another's bedrooms.

Night found her ensconced at the great white crescent moon of her databank, an ever-cycling arrangement of displays softly luminescing from all sides. A hundred different angles on the same dull performance: an ordinary-sized crowd throbbing with ordinary unrest, a loop of predictable people shouldering each other and throwing stones.

"What am I supposed to do with this, *friend*?" she asked aloud to the dark, a shivering hiss, her jaw feeling tight.

She pinched the air and a frame drew closer to her, swelling like a monolith in her field of vision. Waved a finger halfheartedly and paused the footage: someone was shoving down front, empty eyed, a raw look of glee on his face. She had body language analysis algorithms, but hardly ever needed them anymore—this person wasn't protesting anything. He just enjoyed an excuse to push people. Bex pushed the frame down the line, called another one, frames spooling past her like the carriages of a train: here, she spotted three people nearly stampeding into the conflict, ignoring a child who had fallen to the ground right by them. Maybe one of them had even pushed the child.

"Friends and neighbors," Bex said darkly. One of the women holding a Free Minds sign had a designer jacket, even though she was trying to look tough, populist. The display told Bex the label name and the price tag. Often, she saw criminal record flags sprout into being, blood-red arrows that dangled sharply over the heads of the people on display. Noise violation. Drunk and disorderly. Minor possession. Someone projecting a WE WANT JUSTICE sign had a warrant violation for outstanding child support payments. Bex felt her thin lips twist almost involuntarily into a smile. It was all so predictable. Boring, even. *Community building.*

The stims seemed to slow the footage down, passing blocks of projection frames in slow motion across her gaze, setting each afloat in the black sea of her overlarge pupils. They formed a great spoked wheel of light with Bex at its center, displays looming like sanctuary walls around her. If only Jackson Howard and his awful team could see this. Could understand. Or maybe he'd just feel sorry for the criminals. Their neighbors had failed them, he'd say. We should target them with better product and service algorithms.

Then Bex saw a girl in a green cotton jacket, probably just about college age, pinned between the transplas and the asphalt as the *Sunshine Junction* presenters fled for the security vehicle. She paused the frame, summoned it closer to her. There was something vulnerable about the girl's face, the costume jewelry of earrings and lip rings, the awful, short hairstyle with its bleached ends. Performative coolness; the fear in the girl's eyes was very real. It was a familiar kind of humanity.

"What are *you* doing here?" she heard herself croon through her teeth, catching a flicker of her own mad-eyed reflection in the display. Bex felt a low unbidden urge to watch the character become crushed by the transplas, but instead, frame by slow frame, she saw some kind of panicked resolve enter the girl's eyes. With a word, she slowed down the footage even further, watching for the precise second those gray eyes grew just a little wider, shifted to the left, tracked the infinitesimal movement of her pupil. Then the character reached out her hand, thin arm snaking boldly among the pounding boots, thin fingers grasping at risk. At a PAD, which the display told Bex belonged to NBN.

"*Look* at you," Bex said softly, a high, thin laugh escaping her. She beckoned at the display. It loomed closer and locked the little activist in its center. *Lana Rael, Rutherford Arcology 7.* And there was a little more information—her father was a lawyer, she went to Breaker Bay, she studied communications—but not much more.

"Are you for real?" Bex asked her softly, dimly aware of her teeth chattering a leaden drum roll between her ears.

The display looped, time leaping and yawning, Lana Rael reaching for the PAD, pulling it inside her coat. Then Bex wound the footage backward, so that it looked like Lana was pushing the device away from her, shrinking back under the transplas, the resolve shrinking from her eyes like an injury in reverse.

"Let's find out," said Bex. She hadn't laughed all day, but the sound bubbled up involuntarily from her lips, like sick.

CHAPTER 4

For the second day in a row, Lana especially dreaded her Mega-Buy shift. Fragging "Carol," or whatever she was called, and her little sneers, her looks of naked disdain. She wasn't sure with whom she was more irritated: that girl, with her try-hard hair and predictable attitude problem, or Johnny, for pushing her to ask about the brain-nets to begin with.

"Carol," or whatever, had actually taken her earpiece off and turned around in her chair with a tedious creak. "What makes you think I'd know anything about that?" she'd said, letting her lip curl, her arms folding. Body language assessment: confrontational. Treat the customer with exceptional deference.

"A friend of a friend." Lana twitched one shoulder, diffidently. She'd stolen a glance at the other girl's name tag, which read "Martina." *Ooh, so many different names*, she'd thought darkly. *You're super punk rock.*

"Carol" had raised her eyebrows expectantly.

"Like, on the boards." Lana had sighed. "Sorry. Like, my friend heard about this g-mod, who was a hacker, and I thought, like—"

"*The boards*," she'd replied, hooking twin fingers disdainfully in the air. There had been a long, unreadable pause during which the dyed-hair girl, with her pale, messily lined eyes, had assessed Lana with an unreadable look.

Then the girl had snorted, already turning her chair back toward her display. "Yeah, all great hackers get their start at the fragging MegaBuy. You wish, kid. Get on your fragging vid line before someone writes you up."

Lana felt her cheeks scald faintly whenever she thought back on the conversation. Over the past few days since that interaction, she had arrived for her shift a few minutes early, just so she'd be already busy with her display when the other girl came to work.

"Whatever," Lana muttered aloud in spite of herself, paging through the vid queue for her next customer. "It's not like 'punk' hasn't become as commercial as the ecosystems it once aimed to criticize, anyway."

"Are you still mad?" Johnny tossed over one shoulder. "Ow-owooo, it's a *cat fight!*"

Johnny "Icarus" Milton—no, it was "Johnny Millions" this week—was becoming less a funny person she could count on to break up her shift and increasingly yet another nuisance in her dull wage-slave life. At the end of the month, her father had told her, he would stop helping repay her student loans. The renovated condo-hab at the arcology was already a financial privilege, he said, and she was expected to rise to the occasion. The thought of *two* MegaBuy shifts with just quiet Tim and sneering Carol was unbearable, and being alone with Johnny made Lana wonder why she'd ever believed in his ideas about rubbing elbows with famous revolutionaries in ritzy hotels up the Beanstalk, or whatever.

"Bet you Tim messages us soon," Johnny said sagely.

Lana ignored him as she crossly patched a customer through the Conflict Resolution Tree, wishing she'd just sold the executive PAD in the first place, rather than making Tim go all the way to some grotty corner of Guayaquil to try to secure secondhand brain-nets from randoms.

"Howdy, Lana," the Diversity Otter toy said, smiling from the edge of her pod. She hadn't realized she had been gazing at it. "Wanna know 'bout new movies in your area? Or get yourself a lil' treat from your MegaBuy Shopping List?"

There was something like a light in its eyes, but Lana knew it was only its lenses. "No thanks," she told it as quietly as she could, so that Johnny wouldn't hear.

But Johnny was already standing up, disconnecting his earpiece. At the same time, Lana felt the subtle vibration of her wrist PAD, which read *TIM*. "He got them," Johnny was saying triumphantly, nodding at her, as if it were his own accomplishment, as surely as if he knew she'd been betting against him. "Let's get out of here."

Lana's queue still had customers in it. "We can't just—"

"Come on," Johnny said, rising to his feet and moving toward the exit. No one was looking, really.

Lana, come on, you can't make a difference in the world just by drawing fragging posters and writing slogans.

Lana, this is your dad. I love you, honey, but I need to see you start making your own way in the world. This is for your own good.

Lana grabbed her coat and her bag and pressed briskly behind Johnny, the acid-colored displays forming a vortex of desperation all around her, threatening to keep her in place forever.

It was a long trip down increasingly decrepit Skyway lines, the afternoon red as blood, suffocating light and heat cooking each lonesome midday straggler. Lana, Tim, and Johnny rode in a compartment alone except for the sick urban smell that followed them. They'd never visited Tim's condo-hab before. Johnny had often emphasized how far away it was.

Too worn down by the afternoon heat to speak, they found themselves crunching the gravel silently on the walk up to an Eastside Tenements slab building jammed with crooked little windows and peeling doors, each with its own plascrete balcony. Old-fashioned clotheslines, football flags, plastic toys, and graffiti dotted the complex's multitiered face, and the empty groundcar lot seccams seemed like old, brick-like heads swinging ominously on broken necks.

As Tim unlocked the sad-looking stairwell gate with a scuffed keychip, two sunburned children stared just as sullenly. The friends' footsteps slapped flat echoes through the plascrete stairwell till they emerged again onto another hallway painted in chipping cadet blue. As Tim fumbled with his front door locks, Lana felt Johnny's eyes seeking hers. She guiltily avoided his gaze.

"Mom," Tim called into the dim space with impossible gentleness.

The blinds were drawn, but the small condo-hab was love-worn and clean despite the sick color of the light, the low din of an old-model threedee squawking almost merrily into the space. Tim's mother was propped on a tweedy sofa, a floral duvet draped over her despite the heat. Bird-boned, she almost disappeared underneath it, and the lower half of her body made an unrecognizable shape underneath the blanket. As Tim softly approached the sofa to bend and kiss her forehead, Lana looked away again, letting her eyes fall on the threedee display. The rainbow palette of a custom *Sunshine Junction* ad promised vouchers for home medical supplies with free delivery if you answered a few questions about your favorite daytime courtroom programs.

"These are my friends from work, Mom," Tim said, encompassing Johnny and Lana with a gesture that looked almost proud. "It's John and Lana. We're just going to play some games in my room."

"Hi," said Johnny. "Hi," said Lana a moment later, feeling profoundly awkward.

But Mrs. Lin looked delighted, bright-eyed, her short black hair pulled back with a merry pink clip. "Of course," she said. "You're the ones who share your lunches! Thank you so much for being so nice to Timmy. Call me Cherry."

Tim reddened, bashful, through the pleasantries, and led the way through the small condo-hab to his own room in the back. It was a tiny space, with a sloped ceiling and a lumpy futon, but his hardware occupied a place of pride in the corner: two screens, and a piecemeal but meticulously kept console lovingly decorated with stickers. There were hand-scribbled notes all over the wall.

Tim had scraped, saved, collected, and built it all himself over the years. There was something suddenly thrilling to Lana about this nest of wires, its tiny little lights like signs of life, hidden safely away in a place like this. There was a nobility to it. Maybe they could really do this. They *were* really doing this.

"Whoa," Lana heard Johnny declare, awe tinging his soft breath, and she felt relieved. She didn't know what she'd been so afraid of, with Johnny. That this wouldn't have been grand enough for him? That he would have made fun of Tim?

They sat cross-legged by the console, shoes off, almost as if at a temple. Johnny's pointy knee bounced imperceptibly, and Lana threaded the secondhand brain-net through her fingers. She'd never seen one like it before, and it intimidated her a little.

"It's supposed to feel a little weird, secondhand," Tim warned, locking his bedroom door, pressing his ear to it cautiously. The only sound from the multimed-room was the sound of another daytime soap theme, or maybe another *Sunshine Junction* jingle, the saccharine collage of Netcast noise that was never too far out of earshot anywhere in this city. "You might get a little sick or have trouble controlling yourself, the boards said, but you're supposed to just try to relax and move through it.

"I'm going to be navigating for you," Tim continued, soldiering away from the door. His breath brushed Lana's temple as he knelt between her and Johnny, placing the net, with its weightless, pearl-like nodules, on her head just so, adjusting it. Lana noticed something warm and purposeful in his eyes, and felt comforted.

"I can use the encryption data from the user login on the NBN PAD to get you into one of the *Sunshine Junction* servers that recognizes that user," he said. "I don't know what kind of stuff you're gonna be able to find there, but—"

"It's funny," Johnny said, as Tim adjusted his brain-net gently, "you'd think they'd like, wipe it, or something. As soon as they knew it was lost."

"It was wiped," Tim said, dragging the heavy futon to them so he could sit on its corner, facing the console. An old dust smell filled the air. "But the user's access data was still there, for some reason. They must have thought nobody could use it."

"Are you sure we can't get caught?" Lana asked, suddenly wishing she could see what she looked like, crowned with this diadem of revolution. Maybe she would actually name her avatar, after this. *The Empress. Angel of the Amazon. The Woman in the Green Coat.*

"You absolutely have to be quick," Tim said quietly, scratching at his nape. "If you stick to the plan in-world and don't mess around, you shouldn't trigger any alarms at all."

"How do we know if we triggered an alarm? Like, if we have to like, evacuate the server or—"

"You're the one who's scared now, 'Johnny Millions'?" Johnny already had his eyes closed, but a long furrow ran darkly up his brow, his temples dampening.

"You just gotta care about procedure," Johnny demurred. "Let's get this started."

Lana suddenly felt a rush of affection, like superheated neurons, toward Johnny, a vague and sharp-edged shape smudging indistinctly to her right. "It's finally time, you guys," she said.

Or she wanted to say. What came out of her was a stunning involuntary noise, wet-throated, that felt loud and completely outside her control.

Lana felt her own body seizing, pitching terrifyingly forward, some incredible force pressing her head roughly, or yanking her legs, the same sensation that comes from forgetting potassium tabs in the summer, an ache in the night. Her periphery glitched, and she tasted something dull and metallic on her lips, something with the texture of foam.

Panic strangled her. She had forgotten to ask if you could die experiencing the Network in full immersion. Some slow holo-playback of Tim, bending tenderly over his mother's tiny body on the multimed-room sofa, chugged in slow, disconnected frames across her aching sockets. *Just relax and try to move through it*, she remembered him saying. Lana willed every unbridged synapse to slacken, every jagged nerve to lie flat, every frightened fault line in her utterly childish, useless heart to soothe.

It's just a body, just a human body, she told herself. *You can't save the world with fragging posters and slogans. Move through it. Move through it.*

Black sunspots blossomed behind her eyes, and she could hear a shallow breathing that she thought was her own. A pale artificial light became visible in the corner of her field of view, and she heard an old, familiar tune: the sound of the *NBN News Now Hour*, which always meant that her father was about to come home from work. Lana willed herself toward the light of the display, and suddenly felt herself being yanked forward, the abrupt sting of something swatting at the backs of her legs, a pain that hung there. Where was Johnny?

White lights—was it data?—coalesced at her feet, forming pale bulb-like studs that guided her deeper. Her hands tingled, and she found that she could move them, or think about them.

Collecting the shipwreck of her neurons methodically, clinging to her senses—*it smells like summer lawns, I hear music*—Lana thought about continuing, and so she was continuing. Memory of leaving a theater along a path lit up like this, part of a crowd of people who'd been very excited to see this threedee, some threedee. She had some kind of souvenir toy—

Concentrate, she told herself, focusing on the music she could hear, a toy piano plinking out a familiar song.

"*Sunshine Junction*." Her own voice rushed back to her ears like the hum of an old-fashioned machine, and the arcs of electric light that juddered across her gaze knitted themselves neatly into thin-lined, luminous meshes. It was some projection of the animal friends, overlarge, looming, waving slowly, beckoning. They were standing in a field of flowers—no, cameras, great lens-eyed machines nodding up and down on the stalks, speckling her gaze with tiny lights. At the sight of them Lana felt a cold and sudden terror that simultaneously puzzled her. Why should she be afraid of the *Sunshine Junction* Friends? She tried to recall the Diversity Otter toy on her desk at MegaBuy, except in her memory it suddenly seemed to have a massive, open mouth lined with teeth. It must be the brain-net.

"Come in, come in," the friends were saying, their eyes glassy, among the nodding lenses, spread paws reaching toward Lana, seeming to grow bigger. For long moments she hung there, chilly with a fear she could not explain, wondering if something had broken. Her senses were fried, and she was waiting in line for—what, the threedee? She thought very hard about it, about providing a ticket, or about saying *yes*, and as she did so the sound of the toy piano swelled, the laughter of the animal friends surged, and she felt herself yanked forward again, foreign sensations grasping at her arms, the weird old sound of a shutter clicking hotly across her face, a sound from some forgotten time.

Swept along, fighting for purchase, Lana felt she was swimming uphill, a tiny mushroom-shaped structure of yellow light floating toward her, or she toward it. *That has to be the right direction*, she thought. A *Sunshine Junction* Friend House and memories of the program slunk unbidden into her vision. Just how many times had she watched the silly children's show? *The yellow house belongs to Problem-Solvin' Puppy*—yet another fact dredged up from a dim reserve of *Sunshine Junction* facts that seemed to have saturated her awareness, somehow. *Empathy Cat wants you to consider the needs of others before yourself. Friendship Rabbit reminds us that any relationship can become a friendship. Diversity Otter says not to discriminate. Problem-Solvin' Puppy leads the animals in conflict resolution.*

Suddenly, a hulking shape intruded into her consciousness, inappropriately large: the mechanical guts of a toy dinosaur, most of the green vinyl skin gone, two red lights swimming dully in the eye sockets. Wires spilled forlornly from its maw. It was half terrifying, half sad.

"Go," she heard herself manage, "g-get away."

The terrifying shape flickered like a malfunctioning threedee display and then disappeared.

Lana gained momentum, hurtling toward a great big, round door. A grim, looming rendering of the puppy—headache-pink T-shirt stretched across a swollen belly, chasm-like grin—emerged, filling the space and drifting toward her. Its eyes were two dark holes, like the fiber weave of a speaker. Its mouth flapping was utterly soundless, its focus group–tested cuteness grotesque.

It felt wrong. As Problem-Solvin' Puppy drew closer, tiny red lights blinked on in the hollow eyes. Lana was aware of the halos of other character colors closing in.

Lana pressed forward through the dark hole, the open door to the puppy's house. But there was no interior, just the back of a film set, an unsettling conflagration of scaffolding and paint. In the center was a prop table, and on the table was an oversized, sunshine-yellow folder stamped with a shiny star sticker. Emblazoned on it in red children's marker were the words "SECRET FILE." She felt the fleeting memory of her father knocking at the door to her childhood room, telling her it was time to shut off the threedee.

Suddenly she thought she heard Johnny screaming.

She hesitated just one more moment, then grabbed the file in both hands, almost knocking herself backward, nausea abruptly seizing her just a half-second later. Tim had to be ending the sim: the floor was rushing up to meet her, the floor had ceased existing as a concept—

Her face was oddly wet, and her temples throbbed with stereo noise—a *caw caw caw caw caw* that sounded for all the world like a raven, or her own heaving, still ringing in her ears even as she opened her eyes again.

Chapter 5

The jangle of the desk comm jerked Bex out of the kind of black, woolly sleep that parches the mouth and gives no rest. The speckled wash of artificial lights had just begun to flicker into the artificial environment of her office suite, that colorless hour in between day and evening.

"Yeah," she told the comm, bracing for the likelihood that it was Jackson Howard, *just checking on your progress, friend.* "Ms. Gleeson? This is Bernice Mai." Bex clattered upright, instantaneously forgetting the crick in her neck, the mad curl slowly working itself loose from the front of her taut coif. "You got them?"

"Yes, ma'am."

"All three?" Bex dug her fingernails into her palms, hard.

"Yes, ma'am."

The noise she made was involuntary, a shuddering moan ending in a piercing note, like a sob that quickly sharpened into *yes yes yes yes yes.*

"You're a star, Bernice. Bring me everything."

Bex opened the slenderest drawer of her desk, and with a fingerprint scan, sprung the small, cold little lockbox she found there. She had more than enough stims to get through the night's work. Some part of her parasympathetic nervous system spasmed eagerly just at the sight, although for the first time in almost two years, she couldn't tell whether it was the anticipation of success or the drugs that did it.

She twisted a vial into the applicator and held it to her eye, the spidered wing of her mascaraed lashes arching all the way back, a curtain lifting for the dazzling performance, red snowflaking across her field of vision, tiny peaking lights that ebbed as the chilly sharpness of her own consciousness emerged, pure and hard laser light.

It's time, she thought, with perfect calm, burning chemical tears running out of the corners of her eyes.

By the morning, she had retouched her eyeliner and pulled her hair tightly back, not a single mad curl out of place. She felt aware of a pleasant hiss in her consciousness, a Netcast of dead air.

Everyone was already gathered in the Network Programming Theater beneath the dark monolith of the room's hundred screens—all the executives, all their aides, the vice presidents, the Netcast liaisons, the administrators, the stink of coffee and lackluster Wednesday morning wittering filling the dark room. Silhouetted in the corner, Bex took in a slow, still breath. Her fingers rimmed her sleeves, smoothing them over the pulse points, and then her collar, touching the highest button like a totem, every aspect of her sealed. She had practiced what to tell them. She had whispered her presentation speech rapidly and madly in the dark for hours while editing with both hands.

The spotlights ticked on, one at a time, bathing her in blinding radials of bright heat, rendering her image immense before the theater's hundred-eyed display, before the audience whose shapes she could no longer make out. She could no longer see anything but the light.

"Ladies, gentlemen, and others, as you know, I'm Rebekka Gleeson."

She took her position behind the prism-like front podium, letting her long fingers spread and settle over it almost gracefully. A small Friendship Rabbit toy had been placed on the smooth surface for some reason. Bex felt herself smile oddly. Jackson Howard was sure to be listening—that despised, grinning friend.

"As you know, I've been executive programming lead for Global Adaptive Entertainment Netcasting Solutions for six years now. My group has been crafting disruptive content innovations that challenge the boundaries of what our viewership expects from its media, leveraging NBN's massive surveillance network to tailor unique, personal interactive experiences that surprise and delight consumers, and give them precious insight into the daily lives and concerns of their friends and neighbors.

"Yet it's insufficient merely to innovate," she said, raising her voice. "We must *lead* innovation. As all of you know, we are in an era of civil unrest, and now, more than ever, our Programming Department must rise to meet a crucial challenge: our viewers— our *participants*—in New Angeles want to feel safe. They want the tools to protect themselves and their neighbors. They want to know that NBN is watching over them, as we have always done."

She paused, tonguing her lip. On cue, the hundred-eyed monitor bank sprung to vivid life behind her, airing looping footage of the mobs surging forward toward the *Sunshine Junction* holos, throwing stones, tearing circuits. A scene of feral unrest: *The Incident.*

"Especially in times of unrest, we find ourselves asking *why*?" Bex continued, feeling her own heart quicken, a sudden uptick that made her close her eyes softly, her lips frozen in a serene, pale curve. "What makes neighbor turn on neighbor? Can these violators teach us something about why this happens? Can we engage our community in this study, to foster the kind of collaboration that will make our world a better, safer place? As Mr. Howard says, an informed neighbor is a moral neighbor, and we here at NBN are in the business of information."

Bex idly picked up the vinyl Friendship Rabbit toy from her podium and curled her hand gently around it.

"Friends," she said grandly. "Our intimate journeys inside the fashion and entertainment industry are no longer enough to satisfy the educated consumer, and Global Adaptive Entertainment Netcasting Solutions must go further than frivolous escapes from the troubles of the world. We must now empower citizens to choose the best and most positive ways to react to those troubles."

The hundred displays behind her locked upon the paused image of Lana Rael, a colorful spot in the crowd of rioters, hiding under the broken transplas shelter. One hundred crouching college girls.

"This is Lana Rael. She lives in Rutherford, in Arcology 7, and participates in many of our products and services. She's one of our neighbors, as we like to say."

Gently, gently, the frames lurched forward. The room's murmurs fell to quiet attention as Lana's image moved, the skinny arm snaking out subversively, fingers grasping toward the theft of company property.

"She is also our enemy," Bex said, rolling the smooth rabbit toy between her long-fingered hands, feeling the shapes of its ears, as if to soothe it. Pausing for impact.

"Lana is a recent Breaker Bay honors graduate who gets an allowance from her father and works just one MegaBuy shift," she explained, as footage of Lana on her vid line, Lana entering the elevator at the arcology, Lana standing outside the service center on a PAD call with her father, looking petulant, spun across the manifold monitors.

The images multiplied, diversifying across the massive monitor bank behind her. "Yesterday, she and two of her friends engineered a terroristic electronic intrusion into one of our own marketing data servers for *Sunshine Junction*. They used black-market equipment and stolen hardware to plan a sophisticated information theft, and they very nearly succeeded."

Silent footage of Lana, John Milton, Tim Lin, crossing the MegaBuy parking lot, the images flicking past in lazy slow motion. Footage of the friends in a bar called El Puma, toasting one another. Their mouths made natural, voiceless movements on the recordings, doubtless sinister collusion. In the editing she had desaturated their faces to an optimal extent, giving them the haunting look of crime films.

"Here, we have an unprecedented opportunity to understand the mindset of our antisocial populations. And finally, we can go further than asking our community to be good neighbors to one another— we can show them that there can be consequences otherwise."

Dead silence in the room. Bex squeezed the Friendship Rabbit toy in her fist.

"Friends," she said, hearing her own voice resonate and swell, filling every corner of the room, "let me present my midseason replacement proposal: *Desperate Young Activists of New Angeles.*"

The monitor bank exploded with a stellar burst of close-ups taken from inside the washroom mirrors of every New Angeles public restroom that the three had ever used. Johnny, practicing his grin, his pose. Fingerguns. Tim, eyes downcast, dutifully drying his hands. Lana leaning close, rotating her lip ring so vividly Bex felt the room wince.

"These lost sheep have the opportunity to cause genuine harm to our populations. For the first time, we'll have an unprecedentedly intimate look at their daily routines, their habits and beliefs. Thanks to their existing relationship with our network of community-oriented products and services, we'll have a never-before-seen look at the unglamorous reality of unproductive dissent. We're asking these agitators to exchange their privacy for the edification and betterment of all."

"A good neighbor has nothing to hide, after all," she added, a drawstring pulling up her smile, the curled lips of someone sucking on a lemon.

A murmur of approval surged through the crowd like a wave, and Bex rode it, gripping the toy rabbit in one hand, the edge of the podium in another. "Each episode will be generated in real-time from surveillance footage to which, as residents of New Angeles, our subjects have already volunteered their consent. All citizens depend on our products and services, and have signed end-user license agreements that allow us to determine how we use their information. It's an untapped reservoir of raw human portraiture, and it's all completely legal and ethical.

"For example: as an employee of MegaBuy, which uses NBN's Network to provide its customer satisfaction and fulfillment tools, Lana and her co-conspirators' employment contracts include permission for full-scale on-site surveillance. As a Rutherford Arcology 7 resident, Lana is an automatic subscriber to our Netcast and connectivity service packages, which record her movements and her buying habits."

The databanks: Lana at work, Lana facing her vid station, sulkily. *"Thank you for vidding MegaBuy. I'm Lana; how can I help you?"* Lana in the arcology's plaza-level pharmacy, comparing feminine hygiene products. A brief, salacious flicker: Lana's shape through the doorway of her bathroom at home, reaching for a towel. Lana at home, on the couch, eating cup ramen, immersed in the pastel-colored soft light of her threedee.

"As you can see, it looks like she watches *Sunshine Junction!*"

An explosion of vigorous laughter and applause from the room, which Bex shouted over, her throat taut, adrenaline and the echo of the stims thrilling up her razor-straight spine. "For the first time, Global Adaptive Entertainment Netcasting Solutions will not merely be creating entertainment. This is more than just one show: across *all* our channels, we'll be performing a crucial public service, a living behavior study of terrorism and, we hope, a significant deterrent that will be cast multiple times per day across *all* our networks! Friends, fellow executives, I am asking you to greenlight this revolutionary new series *today*, right here and now. Let's *make* the news, NBN. Let's make Netcasting *history!*"

Thunderous applause. Blinded by the light, Bex could only make out a dark wave of silhouettes rising, their black heads floating upward, each ovation a certain approval.

She was grinning, jaw screwed shut, humming like a live wire. She didn't realize she had twisted the Friendship Rabbit toy in her hands until its head had come right off, the wire entrails dangling from her two triumphantly raised fists.

CHAPTER 6

I think we actually got away with it."

Lana still felt something like a hangover, an odd sort of looseness between her thoughts that made her temples ache. She'd thought about calling out of work, but with Tim staying home to analyze their score she worried about looking suspicious. The hated acid-orange vid display swam in her field of view, loading the next ten minutes of her queue.

She became aware that Johnny had been whispering something. "What?"

"I said, I think we actually got away with it," he whispered loudly.

Last night after they'd come to, neither of them had been so sure. Tim said they'd almost had their connection routed back to their condo-hab, and for long minutes Lana felt stunned, like the world around her was being mistranslated somehow. She had lain on the floor with her eyes shut, trembling inexplicably. When it became clear no harm had been done to them bodily, and their senses began to sync with logic again, Tim began to study the data scrap they'd apparently managed to obtain. It would take a long time, and he would need the right kind of help, he said.

Johnny'd sat on the floor, head between his knees, panting and making weird noises, something between a dry heave and a sob. They'd sat in the dark, as if even switching on a light might call some unwanted secguard from the outside, and Johnny and Lana had returned to Rutherford on separate lines, utterly paranoid. Every NAPD officer, every dark suit, nearly gave her the cold sweats, a deep fear that didn't ebb even when she'd returned to her condo-hab in Arcology 7 and shut herself safely in.

She had slept poorly, staring at the indistinct phantasms her eyes had conjured across her bedroom ceiling. In that bleak, drained night she felt she no longer cared whether they'd found any sellable data or not, or whether she had *smashed the state*—probably dinged it at best. It no longer mattered. *Just let this sickness and fear pass and I will be a good citizen*, she promised the darkness. *I will be a good neighbor. If we don't get in trouble, I will send out more job applications. I will get a real job at a nonprofit. I will move to the Valley and become a designer. I will design posters for bioroids' rights*, she thought, with a panicked flicker of hope. *I will pay back my own student loan.*

When morning came, though, it felt like a fresh day, as if the horror had simply been part of a bad dream. Had she really been crouched on a bedroom floor in Eastside last night with a hated brain-net? Johnny's tortured scream, Problem-Solvin' Puppy looming in the doorway of a playhouse movie set? Just yesterday? None of it felt real. Only her buzzing headache lingered to remind her, like the echo of a bad college party.

What if it really *had* worked, she thought, undressing in front of the morning news, oddly calm as she washed the night away in the shower. It was not as hot as usual in the morning, and there was something blissfully unremarkable, orderly, and familiar about the sterile customer service pods of MegaBuy, everyone in their right place as she came to hers, Diversity Otter smiling from the edge of the desk.

"I feel bad about Tim missing his shift again," Lana said, flicking a still-damp tendril of her too-short hair away from her temple, fitting in her earpiece. "It's not like we get paid time off."

"We'll buy him drinks," Johnny said, waving his hand. He was wearing mirror shades at work, for some reason. Examining his own image in the display, he put them on, tilted his head, took them off again.

"Carol isn't here today either," Johnny said, glancing in the direction of her empty service pod. "Or Susan, or whatever."

Lana rolled her eyes and took a call, setting her face in a ritualized expression of pleasantness just before it connected. "Thank you for vidding MegaBuy. This is Lana; how can I help you?" One way or another, she determined, she was going to leave here soon. One day, she was going to make her last route through the Conflict Resolution Trees. There was going to be a last time, and then she would never see the Conflict Resolution Trees again.

"Howdy, Lana," Diversity Otter said sweetly. "When was the last time you took a yoga class? Want me to find one in your arcology?"

"No thanks," she told it.

"Are you talking to the surveillance mascot again? The very symbol of everything you're risking your safety to resist?" Johnny swung around in his chair, giving her an aggrieved look. Didn't he have customers in his queue?

"You know, everything you say and do is recorded here," she reminded him when she had finished.

Johnny rolled his eyes grandly. "For quality assurance," he said, punctuating himself with heavy finger quotes. "I'm a man of quality. Quality gentleman, Lana. Johnny 'GQ' Milton. Oh, man."

"Just do your queue," Lana said, suppressing a laugh despite herself. "We'll have to take some of Tim's today to keep the star rating up on our line."

Hours passed in acid-orange, cotton-mouthed headache silence. No message from Tim, but perhaps he would wait until they got out of work. For safety. *If you never look at the time,* Lana reminded herself, *it goes faster.*

A vicious knot of midday hunger signaled to her that it was probably close to lunch. But when she removed her earpiece, Blinton, the gray-haired supervisor, was standing near her pod. He almost never emerged from the back office, but was perpetually red-faced and harrowed with the labor of his day nonetheless. Lana glanced in his direction and then away avoidantly.

But he extended his arm, blunt fingers crooked, and beckoned brusquely. Startled, she rose and sidled off her line, wondering what could have warranted such a summons. She'd never been written up—she brushed her face with her fingers discreetly to be sure she had remembered to remove her lip ring, and she had. There was no way the MegaBuy customer service supervisor would have any idea about what they'd done yesterday. There was no way. *Oh, she realized, he must want to know why we left early yesterday.*

"Why did you leave early yesterday?" the boss asked, sitting down at his desk, across from Lana, with a creak. The tiny, windowless room smelled mildewy and was paneled in corkboard festooned with blossoms of meaningless little notes. The lingering headache and her hunger made her feel surly.

"Oh, ah," *the story was,* "Tim Lin, who works on my line? His mom has a spinal disease, and I was helping him bring her some home equipment. Sorry—my shift was almost over and it was kind of an emergency, sir. Won't happen again."

She expected this to ease his expression. She was a four-and-a-half-star customer service representative, after all.

It did not. "You know you're lucky to have a position in the MegaBuy family, don't you, Ms. Rael? Jobs for people with no professional experience whatsoever aren't exactly growing on trees in New Angeles these days."

"I know, sir," she recited. "I really appreciate the opportunity to provide customer care for such an essential organization."

"Well, from where I sit, I think you have some problems appreciating your opportunities," the supervisor said, sounding soft and almost wounded. He turned his display to face her, and Lana felt her guts drop. It was her own image, green coat and indecisive hair, in the plaza outside the service center just a few days ago. She looked tiny and out of place, something blown up from the undercity and pinned inappropriately to the MegaBuy's skyscraping call center.

The supervisor knit his short fingers, sighed, and frowned as the recording played.

"*I know,*" Lana-on-screen was talking to her wrist PAD. To her father. At first Lana was startled to see her own image. Then, slow dread, as she remembered the conversation she'd been having in this moment. "*It's not like my life's ambition has been to work at the fragging MegaBuy, Dad. It totally sucks. I've sent out two other applications. Please can we just finish out the month on my allowance?*"

"'The fragging MegaBuy,'" Blinton quoted imperiously, pausing the feed and slowly folding his arms. "You know, I joined MegaBuy as a service representative just like yourself, and I worked my way up the line to regional operations. It wasn't always fun work, but it's important to the company. Do you feel you're destined for *better things*, Ms. Rael?"

Lana averted her gaze, letting it hang on one of the supervisor's wall plaques. Four Quarters Four Stars Achievement Recognition Award: Paul Blinton.

"Oh, no, of course—I mean, my dad's just, like, I have school debt, and he's been, like, really pressuring me about like, my future and stuff, so I was just saying whatever—"

"You never applied for an additional shift," he said, squaring his shoulders at her and hunching over his clasped hands. "If you had, I would have strongly considered you, even though I currently have more applications than I have pods per shift."

"Thank you," she blurted, unsure what else to say.

"But you sent out applications to other corporations." He looked grave, and triumphant at the same time. "What corporations?"

"No, just…a reception job at the Animal League and, uh… part-time canvassing for Opticon Foundation." *Don't squirm*, she told herself. The canvassing job was a volunteer project, but might lead to a semipermanent administration role, the ad had said.

"What's the reason for those choices?" Blinton screwed up his reddish nose and frowned. "Surely the compensation packages aren't up to MegaBuy standards."

MegaBuy standards. Lana felt herself make a sour face before she could stop it. "Some people care about other things than that," she shrugged.

"*Some people*," Blinton said. "People whose fathers pay their rent, I imagine. We're done here, Ms. Rael."

"I can go back to my pod?"

"Of course not. You're fired."

Lana felt color rush to her cheeks. She'd never been fired for anything, never been the subject of disciplinary action at university or at any other part-time job. "What? Isn't there something I can do to—"

"I'm afraid not, Ms. Rael. For some reason this surveillance footage was flagged by SYNC and has been circulating among our execs. Everyone's disappointed that this opportunity wasn't up to your standards."

Blinton pressed something on his desk, and a uniformed sec-man entered to place a small box of things on the desk in front of Lana. It was everything she'd had in her pod: some old facial jewelry she'd forgotten, the unused five-credit MegaBuy gift card she had received as a "joining bonus," a toothbrush, her Diversity Otter. Seeing it lying face down among the junk gave her a twinge of odd guilt, and she found herself gently rescuing it, tucking it into the big front pocket of her green coat.

"Good luck with your next position," Blinton said, ruddy and dour faced and probably secretly thrilled. "Your termination agreement will be sent to your PAD."

Stung with humiliation, faintly dazed, Lana picked up her shoe-box of detritus and followed the secman out of the back office in a long march across the hated orange, transplas service line as the other reps stared. She caught Johnny's eye and thought she'd talk to him, but as she slowed down, she felt the guard's gloved hand propelling her by the nape of her neck.

What happened? he mouthed, and she offered a small shrug, a tilt of her head, mouthed *El Puma* in reply as she hastened past. Johnny nodded once, but he still looked stricken as she left the building.

The long plummet down the familiar elevator felt symbolic, somehow. Outside in the too-clean, climate-controlled halo of MegaBuy Plaza, she watched other employees strolling the grounds in their uniforms. She was an interloper now. She tipped her box of meager property into a bin, which hissed serenely in reply, and picked up the pace, unbidden tears stinging her face, the scald of humiliation still hot.

How did that even happen? she found herself wondering, her feet following the familiar course between the office and El Puma, dully realizing it would probably be the last time she walked this route. *Flagged by SYNC? Why?* Would she still stay friends with Tim and Johnny if they didn't work together every day? What would she tell her dad? How was she going to find a new job when her employment record would say she was *fired* from a fragging *MegaBuy call center*?

The only thing worse than walk-of-shaming away from a Mega-Buy would be crying while doing it, Lana resolved, steeling herself. She would have a drink and some food and wait for Johnny and talk it out and think about what to do. It was going to be fine, she thought. Things were going to work out somehow. She would just have to keep a positive attitude.

It was early enough that there was no one in El Puma besides a couple of the familiar regulars. Lana sat down at a table and ordered a whiskey soda and a seviche plate. She'd planned to just eat the free peanuts to save money, but all the stress and the walking had made her hunger unbearable. She deserved some comfort, she thought. She would start saving tomorrow.

It was also early enough that the *Sunshine Junction Lunchtime Show* was on. Lana watched in spite of herself, half afraid of seeing some record of her invasion. Yet it was business as usual in the merry neighborhood, the four animals untouchable, singing their paw-in-paw welcome tune. It was stupid to be worrying about invasive market research and expensive toys with cameras in them when New Angeles was in the midst of an employment crisis, anyway. *The economy is falling out from under average citizens like me,* Lana thought, sipping her drink.

Doofus Dinosaurus had not chopped down as many trees as the other animals. *"Why are you such a doofus, Dinosaurus?"* *Poor Dinosaurus,* Lana thought, scrolling through her FriendNet account on her PAD. Another girl from Breaker Bay was getting married already. The husband's profile showed he was a few years older, and worked somewhere at a subsid of the Weyland Consortium. *Probably minted,* she thought, flipping sullenly through pictures of the former classmate's expensive-looking wedding.

Lana's own avatar was from graduation day, smiling and triumphant. It was her most recent picture, because nothing good had happened since then. *What a bad week,* she posted obliquely on FriendNet. There would be one or two *omg what happened*s to ignore in the next few hours, at least.

She felt a little drunk already because she was so hungry. Why was the seviche taking so long? How long would she have to sit before Johnny came? How come Johnny never worried about working only one MegaBuy shift? Was Johnny's family rich? Should she marry Johnny?

"Howdy, Lana," said a tiny voice. Momentarily bewildered, Lana realized she had forgotten the toy Diversity Otter in her pocket, and stealthily looked around her to ensure nobody could see her place it on the table. It was a merry-looking thing, paws on its belly, sculpted smile warm. "Are ya havin' a fun day?"

"No," she told it quietly, frowning. Past feeling silly, she tried: "I got fired from work today and I don't know what I'm going to do with my life."

"Cheer up, neighbor," it said, almost gently. "Wanna look at some job listings together? Just tell me three of your best skills."

A sudden lump swam up into Lana's throat.

"Why not join your friends on the *Sunshine Junction Lunchtime Show*?" Diversity Otter suggested. "I can make a threedee for ya right from my tummy-button!"

Lana hadn't realized the toys could do that. She looked at the holo that was already playing and saw the animals had formed a musical circle around Dinosaurus, who looked inexplicably delighted to be sung to about labor. "*Dinosaurus, we're not done! After work's the time for fun!*"

Lana's Diversity Otter toy was singing tinnily along. It was loud, so she put it back in her pocket right as the waitress returned. The disappointing fourteen-credit seviche plate she placed on the table had a faint odor.

Lana carried on drinking in the afternoon, enduring the strange sense of being surgically removed from the productive world, holed up alone in a bar while others worked, bustled past the El Puma window. She was miserable, tipsy, and too hot by the time the distinctive blood-red tinge of dusty sunset filtered through the windows.

"What the heck happened?" Johnny bustled in loudly, swinging his bag onto the back of the seat opposite her and mounting it almost aggressively.

"I don't know." Lana spread her fingers helplessly. "Some surveillance thing. They had me on the phone in the parking lot complaining to my dad about working at MegaBuy and applying for other jobs."

Johnny gave her a puzzled look. "But that footage is just for security. It's weird they would have just come across it, out of hundreds and hundreds of hours, right?"

"Yeah, weird," Lana said. "Yeah, so, it wasn't to do with...you know, the Thing."

"Right," said Johnny. "Sucks, but you'll be fine, right? Your dad has money."

"I—"

"We should vid Tim, anyway," he added.

"Here?"

Johnny shrugged at the two dusty bar regulars, their backs to them. "It's fine," he said, placing his PAD on the smoggy little table. "We'll vid him on mine."

"Hey," Tim's image came up quickly, the dark surroundings of his mother's condo-hab framing an expression that was particularly flat, even for him. "It's not really a great time. The Thing just doesn't seem like anything, and my mom's nursing clone didn't show up."

"Just didn't show up?" Lana said, suddenly feeling odd.

"I don't know," Tim said. "They said there's no record of payment for the past few months, but that can't be true. Our account has some weird sort of SYNC flag on it? I dunno."

"I got fired from work today because of some 'flagged by SYNC' surveillance," Lana admitted, and then turned to Johnny expectantly.

"Maybe something's going on after all," Johnny said, his jaw slackening. "Maybe we didn't get away with it."

"Is...isn't SYNC owned by NBN?" Lana began.

"Timmy," Mrs. Lin's voice called from somewhere behind him in the dark room. "Is that your friend on threedee?"

Johnny and Lana looked up toward the virt hanging over the bar. It *was* Lana, at eighteen, being escorted out of a campus club for...what had it been? Drinking underage? She had almost forgotten until she saw herself, with the shaved head, looking ridiculous and unruly and sloppy and small.

MEET THE HEROES OF TODAY, the screen said in large, bold letters. A frowning Empathy Cat was emblazoned alongside the headline, and there was caption that made Lana's guts drop: RICH RIOT GIRL THIEF HAS CHECKERED PAST.

Johnny stared at Lana. He stared at her like she'd caught something. The lean arc of his body pulled ever so slightly away from her.

"I, ah..." Lana heard herself say softly, tugging at the faint ends of her hair as if it were still long enough to hide her face. She felt suddenly dizzy, as if she were dreaming. As if she were porous.

"You guys, I don't think we got away with it."

The El Puma hostess who welcomed them every day was standing there, staring at them. The two dusty regulars slowly turned around.

Chapter 7

Once a year, everyone in the Programming Department at NBN had to perform a survey on each fellow department member, including executives. *What is your impression of your colleague's work ethic? What is your impression of your colleague's attitude? Which colleague would you choose to work with on a project requiring attention to detail? Which colleague would you choose to work with on a project requiring effective communication? Can you list three achievements of this colleague that have impressed you? Choose the colleague from this list who most needs to improve their conflict resolution skills. Have you invited or would you invite this colleague to your home? Why or why not?*

The Cumulative Perception Index, according to the Human Resources Department, was an important tool to help employees understand how their work was seen by others and to suggest, through crowdsourced data, areas in which they might need to strengthen personal attributes or improve relations with team members. It was absolutely not used to measure performance against determined role metrics or to influence compensation—not formally, at least.

A display panel in radiant burnt orange bisected with vivid spring-yellow lines blossomed idly to life in Bex Gleeson's peripheral vision, showing a trend line that soared and then descended lonesomely away. The trend line's peak coincided with the launch of *Miranda Rhapsody: Pieces of My Soul*, and the line varied almost playfully thereafter. Other lines, like wrist veins, blossomed alongside it: Attention to Detail (ATN), Effective Communication (COM), and Conflict Resolution (CON) swelled and then declined, a symphony of what everyone else thought.

The data set was labeled "Cumulative Perception Index: Rebekka Gleeson (Lifetime)." A prompt on the virt asked whether Bex would like to see individual (anonymous) comments. She had already read them many times in the last year: *Passionate innovator with her finger on the pulse of what drives user relationships with entertainment media. Dedicated visionary with impeccable project commitment and organizational skills.*

And then, the recent year's: *I sometimes question her commitment to the department's greater good. Occasionally self-focused to an undesirable extent. Attention wanders during one-on-one time. Office attendance erratic. Frequently interrupts.* Any of the smiling colleagues she saw every day could have written those.

She did not want to reread the comments today. It was late, and she was alone in her garden of light. Outside the night would be reddish, sulfur scented, the mass of the day's noxious summer heat still hanging, making the steel and glass of Rutherford gray and wet. Here, in the luminous, upholstered silence, she would never see another soul, never have to pretend to smile, never utter a useless word. She thrived here.

Behind her were the thousand faces of Lana Rael, everything SYNC could flag, stretching back years. At Bex's pale left hand, a panel depicting Lana, with a newly shaved head, at a university demonstration against manipulative advertising practices that targeted women. Her lips were moving in silent passion, the sound stripped away. At Bex's right hand, an uncomfortable close-up from Lana's MegaBuy pod, which had captured her during a particularly indulgent eye roll. Waving her fingers almost as if to music, Bex trimmed the vid to the precise excellent moment when the girl's customer service smile fell away like a mask, and the gold-flecked gray eyes launched sideways and then up, the nostrils flaring in disgust at her situation.

"Splice aud," Bex told the dark, and something on her console flickered with warm obedience, as Lana's voice filled the room, a snippet of a voice conversation culled from sometime in Lana's first year of school. *"…was put in Level 2 English by mistake. Maybe I should just stick with it,"* she said, laughing, *"like, I'll look good because everyone else is so stupid. I mean. I'm just kidding, I—"* Bex spread her fingers over the audio console. Snipped the laugh, brought the voice volume down, lower, giving the sound a tinge of warm darkness. *"I'll look good because everyone else is so stupid,"* Lana said again, her words hanging in the dark, synchronizing perfectly with the languid eye roll.

Color correction on the student demonstration vid. Enhance the green of the university lawn, the lush paddock-color of Breaker Bay's idyllic grounds. Make the sky a little bit bluer, and Lana herself a little grayer, a little sadder, a blot on the lucky day. Slow down the eye roll, enhance the unkind curl of the lip, let the viewers really see Lana wear politeness like a lie she could suddenly drop.

Data from one of Lana's beauty store receipts began to march neatly across the bottom of the edited images. A lipstick color called "Revolutionary Red." Something called "Party Eyelashes," which cost twenty-five credits.

The receipt was from a different year, but that wouldn't matter to the viewers.

Bex sighed, angled her head back in her seat, pulling her eyelid back with her fingertips, holding the stim applicator to her staring eye. There was the hiss and sting, a proliferation of red spatter that she quickly blinked away, a thousand rainbow prisms dangling on her eyelashes, fragmenting the endless undersea light of all her media feeds like a beautiful kaleidoscope. A sense of great hunger bled into her limbs, a sense of urgency that was paradoxically soothing, the natural order.

"People are awful," she sighed, her thin lips curling open into a smile that could have belonged to a Netcaster, in another life.

CHAPTER 8

It's a real tragedy, some of these young people today," Paul Blinton was saying on the projection, frowning. "Disrespectful behavior. MegaBuy simply can't employ these kinds of pranksters and terrorists. We had to let them all go."

The footage of Lana finally ceased its merciless loop, replaced by a slow, heavy pan across Tim's condo-hab bloc, which looked squat and lonesome in the eye of NBN's omnipresent cameras. A figure in profile, wearing a bright-pink hair clip, was visible in the window. Cut to a man in the parking lot, emblazoned with the caption *NEIGHBOR*, who looked excited to be on camera. "Tim Lin was working double shifts to support his mom," the man almost gloated. "I never thought he woulda done something bad, but you just never know."

Next Lana saw the interior of her own bedroom on the projection hanging over the bar, saw the custard-colored slice of light coming from her own bathroom, her own silhouette flickering across it. The bad fourteen-credit seviche revolted in her gut, and wildly, absurdly, she found herself thinking *is that really what I look like* and *god I wish my hair would grow out.* Her cheeks scalded, as if with the onset of fever.

"It is you," the sweet, wax-faced El Puma hostess said, looking at Lana and Johnny. Her blank eye, her unerring smile, suddenly felt starkly artificial.

"We gotta go," Johnny said, tapping his ID to the payment panel on the table, flipping its light from red to green. The graphite-colored lines of El Puma's interior, the spotty old bar, the dusty aquarium, suddenly seemed alien, their lights lurid. The world was the same, and yet not. A trickle of humid sweat crawled at Lana's hairline.

"...along with showman 'Johnny Millions' and poor little rich girl revolutionary Lana Rael, both Breaker Bay grads," a breathless, spray-tanned young television host in a tight Problem-Solvin' Puppy T-shirt and black jeans orated as she walked casually down a New Angeles street, hands spread urgently. "These poor misguided kids think they're heroes in a crisis of corporate oppression—and they are making your world less safe. Let's take a walk through the tragic and often hilarious world of modern *slacktivism*..."

Lana recognized the host's background. She was walking down the street near here, near MegaBuy. Almost as if she were on her way.

"You kids couldn't find a real job?" One of the work-uniformed regulars said, a look of naked distaste on his face. The other one shook his head darkly.

"We gotta go," Johnny said, or maybe he'd only said it the first time. Lana felt odd, on delay, like when they had worn the brain-nets, and she turned the collar of her coat up as if to hide in it. She followed Johnny's long, jangling strides out onto the sidewalk, hustling into the crowded evening, the noise of commuters. Every set of eyes that turned their way felt like a searing brand; Lana felt almost lightheaded, stricken, the fever of something like shame entering her face. Was her father watching the Netcast? She hardly even *remembered* getting kicked out of that club in college.

I'm not a bad person, she found herself inexplicably repeating, lips moving softly to herself. *I'm not a bad person, I'm not a bad person.*

There was a camera outside of El Puma. It ticked and whirred like an eye, almost alive, clacking in its socket and turning to face them. The glint of another one winked from farther down the sidewalk.

"Keep your head down and act normal, and we can hide in plain sight," Johnny said, suddenly picking up the pace.

"Where?" Lana said. All her clothes suddenly felt too small, her damp skin too visible. It was suffocating.

"Send Tim a message to come meet us at Broadcast Square. Everyone will be watching the screens, not us."

Broadcast Square was a blossom of sudden radiance erupting from the far end of some dark, glistening urban corridor of Rutherford. Dim office fronts abruptly gave way to an unrelenting fountain of white and gold light, surging noise pollution, and sunshine-yellow beacons undulating optimistically. The city's hub was packed at every hour of the day and night with commuters and tourists, every square inch of glistening metropolis covered with advertisements, news feeds, stock tickers, jingling, chiming, jockeying for the eye and ear. At its center was a surreal, almost alien-looking edifice, a gilded altar that loomed inescapably: a riot of gigantic satellite dishes cupping the heavens plaintively.

Tim had met them at a YucaBean kiosk, red-eyed, pale, and trembling a little, and the three of them clung close in silence, keeping to the dark side of the sidewalk, pressing urgently onward. They had walked almost all the way, fearing public transit, its bright, confined capsules lined with virt displays doubtlessly still showing their faces. Although night had fallen, the temperature hardly had, yet. The assault of artificial light from Broadcast Square was surreal, practically daylight, silvereen and pure.

"Guys, I can't walk so fast anymore," Tim warned.

Somewhere along the way, a red number had started blossoming on Lana's wrist PAD like a wound: FriendNet requests. SYNChat permission requests. Smudged faces, cartoon avatars, looming and grinning. *You are a little fat for my taste*, read a message from jir0214 in Nihongai. *What's up, special snowflake?* said a message from a beefy avatar wearing wraparound glasses, holding a dog. *HOWZ YR REVOLUTION, LOLRIOT?*

"Off," she hissed at the PAD, shaking her wrist hard as she paced briskly. It remained illuminated, fused to her body like an ill heart, buzzing constantly.

"Lana, Tim, come *on*," Johnny urged, loping along quickly toward the heart of Broadcast Square, weaving almost elegantly along strangers who, faces upturned to the spectacle of media, indeed did not pay them much mind. They hustled through a corridor of pastel light, sidestepping to avoid awed children among enormous projections of the *Sunshine Junction* Friends on the facades of buildings, waving mutely. Distorted music came from everywhere, neighborly tunes layering discordantly on top of each other.

"I can't leave my mom all night," Tim puffed. The gentle boy had a panicked look, like he might just bolt into an alley and stay there. Lana, conflicted, walked at his pace and thought of reaching for his hand, but the constant soft buzz of her PAD against her pulse point made her feel almost unclean.

"Come *on*," Johnny said, pulling his collar up, diving into the thick of the crowd. Lana trailed behind, fixed on the suddenly insurmountable number of unread messages, unaddressed notifications, a minefield attached to her body.

Where r u Lanna? and *some1 should teach this young lady respect for the working class.*

"OFF," she barked brokenly at the PAD. Probably the din of the crowd was interfering with the voice controls. Someone nearby started to turn around to look at them, and Johnny grabbed Lana roughly by the arm and hauled her into the flow of human traffic.

"Don't pay attention to that now," he said. "We've gotta get to the big screens."

"It's on every screen," Tim said softly.

Almost as if timed for their arrival, Broadcast Square's enormous virtual displays, its mosaics of visual tiles, fluttered to life, coordinating like a symphony across nearly every surface. They stood in a crowd of hundreds, thousands of strangers with faces upturned, snacks and toys and souvenirs bursting from their arms, religiously rapt. Laser-bright text etched captions across the displays, across the very air itself:

MEET THE UNDEREMPLOYED UNIVERSITY GRADUATES TURNED ATTEMPTED DATA THIEVES. A bouncing Friendship Rabbit head guided the viewer's eye along the phrases.

Johnny was on the screen. On every screen, looming surreal and large, grinning. Tim, carrying groceries across the gravel lot of his East Chakana parking lot, burdened but dutiful. Lana in the public restroom she'd forgotten going to, leaning into the camera—into the mirror—to adjust her lip ring. A collective wince shuddered through the crowd, and Lana found the intimacy with her own face strangely disgusting, the bile of fear building up in her gut again.

They again played the footage of college-age Lana yanking her arm away from a nightclub bouncer, *"my dad is, like, a lawyer—"* She could hear the crowd laugh. The derision in it frightened her. Her SYNChat app tagged her username again and again, a torturous vibration constantly at her wrist. *I better never meet this GIRL,* said a grinning avatar among the constantly scrolling messages. Another: *Her lil cheeks i just wanna squeezem XD!*

She felt like her body was being wedged open, half of it superheated in the pure blazing light of her own giant image, half of it riveted to the crawling infestation of notifications, messages, the sheer overload of information.

"You're invited to join the conversation, friends." The artificially tanned host was on the screen again, this time beckoning warmly, with her whole arm, from some Netcasting studio. "Our advanced technology will find the subjects of this innovative new documentary wherever they are, and you, our neighbors on the street, will be invited to add your *own* found footage to the experience and to win wonderful prizes, product, and service offerings. Your perspective matters!"

A smattering of applause and cheers rang out across the square. Some of it felt very near.

"Maybe we should start running," Johnny whispered. Lana was looking at her PAD.

Got Latest (Uncensored) Arcology 7 Shower Footage xxx Totally LEGAL/Legit enter Y to access
Y
Y
Y

Lana yanked the PAD from her wrist reflexively, hurling it away from her as if it were a live snake. It disappeared into the crowd. A moment later, someone said *hey,* and several people turned around.

"It's them!" said a stranger.

"Welcome, everybody, to *Desperate Young Activists of New Angeles,*" said the host, her voice ringing out off of every surface, and suddenly every monitor changed abruptly to show an image of Broadcast Square itself. To show their own three faces, upturned, staring, startled, whirling and glancing about frantically—uselessly—for the source of the feed. The square was filled with eyes, lenses, people staring, people coming closer.

"Run," said Johnny, beside Lana and on the monitor.

"Run!" shrieked a woman in the crowd, an unpleasantly gleeful bark. Suddenly the people nearest them were pointing their PAD cams eagerly, a flecking of tiny red and white eyes staring in their direction, only their grins distinct among their features in the dark.

Lana was rooted to the spot, unable to stop looking from the big screen to the crowd and back to the screen again. She felt she was going to throw up, on national Netcast.

"Hey," Tim said, showing his palm PAD to Lana. For a dull half-instant she didn't realize what she was looking at, and then she saw it: a closed-channel message, a single unfamiliar, dark window in the middle of the screen.

Alley in back of Silverway and 4th. You have 15 minutes.

The three of them registered the message, met one another's eyes. Then suddenly the screens of Broadcast Square sputtered and went out, throwing the area into lurid, dim phosphorescence speckled with hundreds of PAD eyes, long shadows, and hot human shapes blurring together like smudges on glass.

It was unusually dark. Those virtual displays never went down. An eerie wail surged through the crowd, followed by the long, slow blast of an alarm.

Lana grabbed Tim's sleeve and began to run, shouldering aside two unsettlingly still girls, leering with their slim PADs held up. Inside a luminous electronics store, a crowd had gathered at the window to watch them pass, the interior of the shop lined with staring, lens-eyed *Sunshine Junction* vinyl toys. The passersby waved oddly as Lana, Tim, and Johnny hurtled past, as if they were watching a parade, delighted to be part of the public spectacle. The sound of the crowd never seemed to get any farther away, and every time she looked over her shoulder, a smattering of strangers was chasing them almost languidly, fast walkers jockeying for a snippet of footage on their PADs, vidcam lights sparkling in the dark from farther back. It was impossible to tell how many spectators there were, or what they would do if they came any closer.

At last Lana felt Johnny yank her shoulder and hustle her into a dark gap between two buildings, a bright-yellow Broadcast Square beacon slicing after them like a searchlight. Lana yanked Tim's sleeve, and something in him just seemed to come loose, as he fell to his hands and knees.

"I can't—I can't keep running, you guys," Tim said, breathing hard. "I think I hurt my ankle."

"You have to," Johnny said, gesturing frantically at Tim's PAD, where the stranger's message softly blinked. "Someone's trying to help us. Is it one of your contacts?"

"I told you I don't really have any *contacts*," Tim said, wincing.

"*The tall one is so cute!*" an indistinct voice nearby was shouting; a speckling of tiny red eyes drew nearer in the dark.

"We don't have many choices," Lana said, anguish and fatigue barreling through her. "They said fifteen minutes. We've gotta make it to Silverway and 4th. Come on, Tim, it's just a few more blocks."

"I can't," he said, and tears welled in his eyes, the stricken expression with which he confronted her, firmly. Lana felt her own nails digging into her palms. Johnny looked at the swarm of vidcam lights drawing nearer, and at Lana, and then they both looked at Tim, and at each other again.

"I kinda have an idea," Johnny said, with a sudden calm that Lana found alarming. "You go."

"Me? But—"

"*Get a picture of the girl one!*" someone screamed gutturally, very near.

"*Go,*" Johnny said. "Get help!"

Only the ferocity of his voice impelled her backward—Tim still looked at her plaintively, or resentfully. A stranger rushed up, and Lana watched Johnny step toward her, out of the darkness and willingly into the oncoming cameras. A sudden mewl escaped from eager onlookers excited to be part of the show, the game. She saw him grin and wave at them, hands spread, his silhouette suddenly unfamiliar, hard-edged in all the PAD light.

Lana took off running, farther into the dark of the alleyway: a narrow space lined with refuse and whistling with stale, bitter air. Panic made her lips and fingers cold, and she wasn't even sure, anymore, which way was 4th Street, how close she was to Silverway. The alarm was still blaring, and the noise of chaos in the unusually dark Broadcast Square still sounded dangerously close. The whis-tling howls of NAPD vehicles had joined the noise collage, and Lana, ears ringing, concentrated on keeping the sound behind her. The alley spit her out suddenly onto Silverway, a broad street lined with game parlors and gambling machines. She almost ran into a bismuth-pink *Sunshine Junction* toy capsule dispenser that hulked beside a shuttered newsrag stand, leaping startled away from it as it greeted her in a thin whistle: "Howdy, neighbor!"

The avenue was lined with cameras, baleful eyed and black as a row of ravens, but for some reason their red eyes were not alight; they did not turn their heads toward her like the ticking insect camera above El Puma had earlier in the day. This must be the right way, Lana thought, running hard into the crush of bodies, shouldering aside the ambling teenagers who might not have even seen the Broadcast Square debut, might not even want to take her picture. Might not. Someone cursed her angrily as she pushed them, someone dropped their steak skewer and she did not, could not look behind her, couldn't speak. Her chest ached.

The junction of 4th Street loomed ahead, its familiar arc of col-ored baubles heralding the way. *Please*, she whispered to herself, *please don't let me be too late.* Where was the alley behind 4th and Silverway? She chose the largest building on the corner and fol-lowed around it, found what was either an alley or a garbage repos-itory, and ran down it, sprinting with everything she had, feeling a sea of eyes closing in behind her.

A glittering shape materialized, hulking in wait at the end of the alley. An unmarked hopper, either rented or stolen. What if it were all some awful trick, part of the *program*? What if she was being summoned by the same kind of people who had been mes-saging her? This sudden fear almost halted her altogether, but she couldn't go back.

The hopper door winged open as Lana ran up on it. Sitting in the driver's seat was a familiar girl, half her hair shaved, stripe-dyed, her hands tattooed, waiting restlessly on the controls. Punk music vibrated from the budget speakers, licks of suddenly disrup-tive noise spilling into the staid urban dark.

"Carol?"

She rolled her eyes. "Get in, luser."

Chapter 9

She called herself MaxX. It was a made-up name, like all the other ones. She had sullen eyes, ringed by late nights and yesterday's mascara. She was a g-mod after all. Lana couldn't believe it.

They were about the same age, but MaxX seemed older, somehow. She had a hard face, a constellation of piercings on her earlobes. Improbably Lana felt, along with everything else—the gratitude, the relief, the sick ebb of adrenaline—that familiar stirring of soft resentment.

"How...did you find us?" she asked, following the other girl in the stiff, spiked jacket and matching gloves through a dark lot toward a tall, nondescript condo-hab bloc not unlike the one Tim lived in. Lana had no idea where in New Angeles they were.

"Anyone can fragging find you," MaxX replied curtly, without even looking over her shoulder. The dismal little building's security lock disengaged at her gloved touch, a bleak buzz, and she flung the door open, expecting Lana to follow into the foyer with its prisonlike row of mailboxes, shabby elevator bay.

"Where are we? Why are you helping us?"

MaxX turned around at the elevator, giving Lana a heavy-lidded look, and thumbed the call button. "Welcome to MaxX Fraggin'

Mansions, milady. I know it's not what you're *used* to, but you can hide out here."

Then she smiled, just a bit, a black-lipped and languid look. "It's not that I'm *helping* you. I'm screwing with NBN."

The elevator chimed and shuddered open with an ominous noise.

"Your carriage, Princess," MaxX added, showing some teeth.

Nicotine-stained and piebald, the one-bedroom condo-hab was barely furnished. Its fixtures wept continually, and a panel was missing from the ceiling, insulation and naked pipe visible. The multimed-room's sliding panel faced out onto a tiny balcony speckled with sad plants, overlooking the parking lot. There was a futon on the floor, a smattering of unmarked prepaid burner PADs, and some tin cans, the kind they often got at MegaBuy, and little else in view.

"Bathroom's down the hall, but stay out of my damn room," MaxX said, opening the squat fridge and taking out a cold canned coffee. Lana could see in its yellow interior that it was mostly empty aside from what looked like another burner PAD.

"This is where you live?"

MaxX raised a brow at her. "I just crash here sometimes," she drawled, leaning back on the countertop by her inked arms. "The rest of the time my daddy rents me a suite in Arcology 7."

"Hey, that's not—"

"I don't give a $#*t," she cut her off, chipped fingernail sharply cracking open the coffee can with a metal hiss. "I don't wanna be friends, and I don't care what happens to you after this. I just wanted to steal a cash cow, and you're it."

MaxX pointed brusquely across the room with a gloved finger, circuitry softly radiant in the black of her palm. A PAD flickered on.

Lana wanted to tell MaxX she was not a cow. But she saw Tim on the virt display, crouching soberly over the sofa where Mrs. Lin had been cheerily reclining just a few days ago. In the dark of his condo-hab, the eerie greenish light from a camdrone made him look haunted, pale. He yanked the curtain shut. A pop-up on the display invited viewers to submit their own reaction vids.

"You were going to be the most fun one to hate," MaxX said, gazing at the screen with something like satisfaction in her eyes, the line of her mouth taut. "Now that you're gone, it's just gonna be this and your other shill friend, and no one wants to watch that."

Lana felt a dull ache lance her belly.

"What are we going to do?" she said softly.

"We? Nothing," MaxX's reply was matter-of-fact, her dark-lipsticked mouth veiled by the canned coffee. "This was a one-shot invitation, Princess. You think it's fraggin' *easy* to bring down the surveillance for the entire Rutherford radius for fifteen minutes?"

The girl paused, and looked Lana up and down with a quick flick of her eyes, like the movement of a flyswatter. "Try it," she added. "I'll lend you that brain-net." A flutter of a low, rusty laugh emerged, almost in spite of herself.

"Did you rescue me just to make fun of me? You don't care what happens to them?" Her voice felt stuck in her throat, a thin sound. A younger Tim and a girl who must be his sister moved like ghosts on the screen in the background, pale images whose purpose she could not divine without looking more closely.

"You keep saying these things: *helping, rescuing, caring.* I think you've been watching too much of that *Sunshine Junction* crap." MaxX pressed the coffee can between her odd hands, giving it a strangled shape, and then she tossed it into the sink with a *clang*, frowning at the yellowing kitchen with its bent panels. Hard shrug, the grim edges of her canines showing: "I just like the idea that some of our *television friends and neighbors* at NBN have to be losing their fraggin' minds right now that I ripped the front wheel off their fragging tricycle."

The other girl's face was difficult to read, the fine expression of her eyes edged in ugly black makeup, partially veiled by the vividly striped edifice of her hair. The hard features, the twist of the black mouth, set in anger as a habit, almost serene in it, although every coarse word tugged at the corner of her lips just a little. Brightly colored adverts played on the quietly wittering virt while she spoke.

"What difference does it make," Lana replied miserably. "There's some kind of flag on me now, so they have plenty of old vid footage they can use. They even have…there must have been a seccam behind my bathroom mirror."

"These lusers don't have fun unless they can see that it upsets you," MaxX said, a dark rinse on her tone, the quickening in her speech betraying her emotion. "They're selling it as some 'portrait of the youth' or whatever, to educate the community, but you're being made a fragging example of. They want to just tear you down to feel better about themselves."

"We were trying to do something good," Lana said softly.

"*Something good*," MaxX parroted. She bent to open the sad, small refrigerator again almost reflexively, as if she thought she'd find something new in it. "You could have just paid back my loans instead," she snorted. "Why didn't you just take your shift line out to lunch, kid?"

"The thing about my dad isn't—"

"I said I don't give a damn," the other girl raised her voice, sharply cutting Lana off. "I don't care about the 'real you' any more than anyone else does. I don't *care* about you any more than you care about me, or anyone other than yourself. Just stay here till this $#*t blows over. No one will be able to find you here. Then when the show ends, you can come out and see if you have any shot left at a life. Sorry, kid, that's all I got."

"Stop calling me *kid*," Lana spoke back, something like panic distorting the sound. "We're the same age."

"Yeah? Then you probably should have grown up quicker." MaxX's voice was clipped, but less coarse. Lana felt as though she'd been slapped, the sting of it echoing in the silence. It was the *Sunshine Junction Bedtime Show*, the animals paw in paw in their color-coded pajamas. "*Let's wish good night to all our friends—*"

"*Off*," MaxX snapped her fingers at it abruptly, nostrils flaring, eyes wide as if she'd seen something obscene. "Can't *stand* that $#*t. I'm gonna have a shower and go back to work."

"At MegaBuy?" Lana replied automatically, numbly. She never knew the other girl worked a night shift too. She thought about when she'd get to tell Johnny. Maybe never.

"No, at fraggin' Oaktown Investments," MaxX threw back, sharp, heavily sarcastic, raising her arms to indicate herself, the lean comma of her body, the threadbare clothes, tattoos blossoming like bruises along her arms. "Don't leave this room. You can watch the PAD but don't touch it, don't touch anything else, for any fragging reason. And stay away from the windows. There are camdrones that come here sometimes."

Lana nodded mutely. There was nothing to touch except for the stack of MegaBuy lunch cans arranged on the counter. Her stomach turned reflexively at the sight of them.

"You can have one if you get hungry," MaxX said, noticing her gaze. They weren't gentle words, but the bitterness seemed to have left them, the curl of her lip directed at something else, something other than Lana after all. "Think of it as a gift from your *MegaBuy family.*"

"Thank you." Lana didn't know what else to say.

"Don't," MaxX called back as the dark of the small hallway swallowed her. A few moments later, Lana could hear the humid hiss of the shower coming from behind the shut bathroom door. She remembered *Totally Legal Uncensored Arcology 7 Shower Footage* and felt a little ill. She sat on the floor, directly facing the burner PAD. It could act as a lifeline to the rest of the world, but how badly did she want one? She summoned the display on.

"You were willing to risk losing the support of your community to pursue this dream," a voice was saying. Johnny was on the screen, strolling through Broadcast Square beside a fashionable woman, who was making an intrigued, compassionate face as she walked alongside. Someone had put a *Sunshine Junction* logo T-shirt on over Johnny's sleeveless, and his Netcast image had been optimized, making him look oddly smooth and waxen, uncanny, slightly unfamiliar.

"What the hell," Lana breathed softly, suddenly exhausted. A collision of warring emotions assaulted her: relief, resentment, loneliness, fear.

"See, I was an orphan," Johnny-on-screen said ruefully, steepling his fingers, glancing down at them deliberately as the anchor nodded along, with gravitas. "I went to school on a full academic scholarship with the hope of studying public advocacy, but I guess the most important thing I've learned is that there's a problem with my generation."

"Mmm," the presenter said thoughtfully, as if she agreed and were equally concerned, although she didn't look much older than Lana. There were onlookers standing nearby, pointing their own PAD cameras at the scene, and they nodded, too. Lana pressed closer to the display, looking for signs of coercion, exhaustion, chemical intervention, kidnapping—anything—but could only see the perfectly hued after-dinner story hour glow of the evening show. Was Johnny really an orphan? Had she ever asked him about his family?

"Don't you feel like the biggest way to make a difference in the world is by, like, focusing on our *neighbors*, like, looking out for each other, keeping an eye on each other, things like that?" The presenter gave Johnny's shoulder a pat.

"I know that now," Johnny said, and smiled a platinum megawatt smile at the camera.

A ticker of selected public messages scrolled in the sunshine-gold beam that lined the display. The window header said *JOIN THE CONVERSATION.* The ticker said: *WHAT A HOTTIE* and *omfg soooooo inspiring! luv it!* and *a fine example to the young men of today and if only more men like him took this approach instead of using violence and destructive actions.*

"Do you think young people today have too many career options, too many opportunities, such that they get paralyzed?" The anchor leaned toward Johnny, speaking smoothly. He had a hawkish profile. "Your friend Lana Rael was an example of that, don't you think?"

"I think so," Johnny nodded almost serenely.

Lana read the *JOIN THE CONVERSATION* window in spite of herself: *do u thnk they were together lmao* and *maybe we find out next week.* So many strangers' names. Someone confidently asserted: *she is most certainly gay.*

"I am not," she reflexively muttered to the screen. Her voice activated an automatic messaging window: *JOIN THE CONVERSATION?*

"No," she muttered surlily, dismissing the pop-up, which materialized as a big *WELCOME* banner waved by Empathy Cat. Lana doubted MaxX would let her have some kind of anonymous account just to argue on her own behalf on the Network. *Fragging Johnny! He had to be under duress,* she thought. She found herself almost hoping so. If this was one of his brilliant plans, Lana couldn't see how it would turn out to be a very good one.

"How do you feel, knowing that Tim Lin was pulled into this— well, we really have to call it *slacktivism,* don't we?"

"Yes," Johnny said, and laughed a little. He was doing humility, self-effacement so well that Lana found it uncomfortable.

"To help you and Lana, and now—"

"Off," Lana barked at the display, which abruptly dissipated. What must her father think, watching this? There was no way she could risk calling him, even to let him know she was safe. A white-hot pain had entered the front of her skull slowly over the last several hours, and the nausea in her gut blossomed in the dead nighttime heat of the unventilated condo-hab. The threadbare carpet had generations-old mildew stink in it. She listened for the sound of the shower to make sure she was still alone, and then she lay on her belly, buried her face and arms in her green coat and cried. The sobs hauled themselves up from the exhausted core of her with force, and even while she muffled them, she was afraid of their volume.

Something hard made a buzzing noise under her cheek.

"Howdy, Lana," Diversity Otter murmured sweetly through the fabric. "Sounds like you're sad. Wanna play in your favorite friendly neighborhood?"

Lana pulled the toy stealthily out of the pocket, letting it recline gently in her open palm. She had just heard the shriek and thud of the shower taps turning off.

"Can you talk more quietly?" she whispered to it.

"Sure can," said the toy, at a lowered volume. Did it...wink? It had to be the light, just playing off the glittering lenslike circle of the toy's synthetic eye.

"Lana, ya know I'm your friend, don't cha?"

CHAPTER 10

I must be losing my mind," Bex Gleeson spoke into the dark theater, licking the stretched parchment of her lips for the hundredth time. There was no one to answer, but she never really allowed anyone into her sanctum. The dozens and dozens of displays sent the distinct pain of a migraine into a point above one of her eyes, where it hung. "It's been days. Why can't we find her?"

There were twenty different angles of Tim Lin rooting around a junk lot in Chakana for spare parts, with homeless people and their junk sticks, and it had been going on for hours and no amount of editing was going to make it less tedious, and at this point the only way it was going to get watchable was if someone started a fight.

Bex touched the console with a skinny, jittery finger, and spoke briskly into it. "Can we get an actor down there in the next twenty minutes to start a fight, please? This scene is putting me to sleep, and I don't have time to sleep right now."

"Sure thing, Ms. Gleeson," some kid chirped back brightly from somewhere, and Bex pressed her fingers to the aching orbits of her skull, finding that the bones of her face seemed to swim more easily to the surface these days. She hadn't felt so sick since the days when she'd been editing the *Miranda Rhapsody* program, which had to bode well, she thought. It had to turn out all right.

Monitor bank one was supposed to be for working with Lana. It was dark, like a knocked-out tooth.

On monitor bank two, a wall of Johnnys modeled several different looks for the *Sunshine Junction* tie-in Jackson Howard had insisted on. According to the program description, he was slated to help the *Sunshine Junction* Friends teach Dinosaurus about cyberbullying, across several different campaigns. It was weird, she thought, how just the littlest bit of comfort and attention had made him roll right over. He made for popular viewing among the desirable market of median-income girls ages eleven to sixteen, but breeding a new human brand hadn't been on her to-do list, and it wouldn't make the show successful on the level the executive board was expecting. It was proving too hard to craft a narrative arc. The plan for the season finale was just refusing to materialize. Unless Tim Lin's mother died or something.

The Tim Lin bank erupted in activity as the appointed performer arrived, blending in so quickly with the other destitutes that Bex soon lost track of them. She watched them fighting, a bigger man against a smaller, and felt the softness of her own mouth hanging like a disconnected wire. She watched and waited to see whether Tim would run or try to help.

"Launch a live poll, please," she murmured to the console. In a moment, a Real-Time Conversation Widget appeared on the display in response to the crook of her finger, and she watched the statistics rack up, the bright golden numbers blinking across fractional data variations like eyes. Sixty-six percent were currently in favor of "help."

Bex's mouth twisted as she watched, listening to her own shallow breathing. On the display Tim paced backward slowly, awkwardly, and then he ran. She smiled.

Something spasmed in her jawline. She held her pinched fingers to the display and pulled, like tearing a flower apart. In realtime, for all the viewers to see, she gently pinned the biometric data from his mother, Cherry Lin, alongside his ruddy face as he puffed to escape the parts lot. The radiance of her pain juxtaposed against the inadequacy of his own physical effort. Everyone would see it like that—*it just doesn't look good u kno*, went one of the messages Bex caught out of the corner of her eye. *lol imagine if yr son was such a luser :x*

She focused on this for so long, reading every message with a jaw-locked, dilated calm, that she hardly noticed a pale baby-blue light flicker on behind her, on monitor bank one.

"...*like, I know there are bigger problems in the world than me not knowing what to do since I got out of college, but, like...*"

Bex whirled in her seat, swimming in the air through slow motion, her aching gaze swiveling slowly toward the single active point of light on the dead array, the control panels blinking softly. She could hardly believe it, actually knuckling her eyes till the dark behind her lid was flecked with black-and-red starbursts, but it really was the girl, just materializing in her dragnet, facing the soft light some device must be shining in her face. The device was also projecting familiar-hued holos around Lana where she sat cross-legged on a threadbare floor, the room around her sad and dark by contrast.

"*Everyone's feelins matter, Lana! Sometimes you just gotta talk with yer neighbor,*" chirped a voice, very close to the recording site.

Bex's jaw seemed to unlatch and hang. *Sunshine Junction?*

"*I had some friends back in Free Minds Club, which is where I met Johnny,*" Lana was telling the toy softly. "*But I guess I went to work with him at MegaBuy because I didn't really have any other ideas. I kept thinking something was going to start happening for me, like it had always just happened, I guess, and I thought I was just gonna keep being good at stuff like I was at school, and now I...*"

She was crying. Diversity Otter was singing softly to her. Bex felt the rapid surge of something like joy thundering wildly in her chest. A soft display reading *GO LIVE?* across a thick, dark-blue button loomed close to her hand, but she waved it away. This was almost good enough on its own. Almost.

"*...and now everyone hates me,*" Lana said.

"Can you trace the location?" Bex spoke quickly into the air, clipped, not wanting to miss a word.

"Sorry, ma'am," came Bernice Mai's voice, coming from everywhere in the editing amphitheater. "It has its parental controls on."

"Just record, then," Bex told the display abruptly. She continued to watch, a strange fascination overtaking her, almost despite herself, a feeling she didn't recognize nudging beneath the soft part of her breastbone.

Chapter 11

The light that bled in through the old drapes was rust colored, the weird hue of neither night nor morning, but sometime in between. No one likes to see that color, hear its attendant thundering buzz, the city grid mostly asleep, sweating in the summer night. Lana lay curled on the hard floor of MaxX's multimed-room, eyes aching with sleeplessness, skin taut with hurt. It had now been a few days since MaxX had last returned to the condo-hab, but Lana often had to remind herself it wouldn't be any better if she were there.

Few words ever passed between them; MaxX always shut herself in her room, the unpleasant tinny grind of punk guitars chugging from behind the closed door as loud as a keep-out sign. Lana could watch mediafeeds. Or, when alone in the condo-hab, she could talk to Diversity Otter.

The worst part of the day was after the *Sunshine Junction Lunch Hour*, when the community shared *Desperate Young Activists of New Angeles* memes. A lot of them were based on pictures and footage Lana had never even seen before. Old images, a sort of patchwork of her life that was partially familiar and yet not. At first she couldn't bear to watch it, some smudge of her face paused mid-sentence from an old school feed, or captured in the lurid light of her own PAD camera, her hair, before she cut it, hanging over her own face. Those kinds of pictures, the ones where she was especially young, were popular in a way she didn't like, the fruits of all the end-user license agreements she and her parents hadn't bothered to read.

Last she had seen, Johnny had been invited to be a contestant on a program where Netcast personalities who had broken the law were locked in a glass box together for forty-eight hours. The box was installed in the middle of Broadcast Square so that people could walk by it and look in person. He had been smiling the whole time, even though it was the dead of summer and the box's interior was misted in a vulgar way, and even though onlookers occasionally threw things. A lot of girls came to take PAD pictures of him. It looked like his shoes were very white and new, and it all made Lana resent him deeply. She wondered if he was getting to rub elbows with famous people in up-Stalk hotels.

MaxX was right, Lana felt. She was being made an example of. It was the fashion to write PRINCESS on her face; there were user-submitted "citizen Netcasts" about political trends that Lana supposedly represented.

"*Everyone else is so stupid,*" she heard her own voice saying, many times per day, and other things, half-remembered snippets, clippings of party gossip, things that just sounded awful and alien on their own. It was her own voice, and yet not. Lana felt a certain gap opening up in her perception of herself: if she recognized the girl on the screen, then she would stop recognizing herself. Or so she thought. In the lonelier times, during those strange-colored hours of night, she wondered aloud if maybe all of this were some momentous incident of revelation, reflecting back at her the previously unknown fact that she was, indeed, objectively a bad person, and had been all along.

"No yer not, Lana," said Diversity Otter, standing by her head in the dark. Lana had never noticed before that the soft mouth moved just a little when it spoke, that the light in its eyes could follow her around the room. "It's just confusin' when everyone's bein' so mean to ya! Remember when we made a list together of all the times you'd been a good neighbor?"

"Yeah," Lana sighed heavily. "But no one else knows about it. They all think I'm a spoiled destructive princess, or something."

"Does that matter?" Diversity Otter chirped back gently. "It's like Problem-Solvin' Puppy likes to say, 'character is who you are when there's no one watchin' at all.'"

"Someone is always watching," Lana sighed. "That's, like, the NBN's entire motto, right?" She couldn't focus her eyes on the display anymore, but she couldn't bear the dark and quiet of being alone, so she kept her gaze fixed on the waxy, subtly animated smile of Diversity Otter.

"What's *yer* motto, Lana?" the toy asked.

"Cameras are bad," she replied sullenly. She couldn't think of a real one.

"Not all of us," Diversity Otter chirped merrily, a whistling laugh that sounded warm, almost organic. "I was thinkin' that if everyone could get to know ya the way I know ya, maybe yer troubles would be solved."

"My only friend is a *Sunshine Junction* toy," Lana mused, repressing the bubble of a weird laugh, extending her arms and resting her head on them.

"You got all kinds of friends and neighbors out there, Lana. You just need to meet them." The toy projected pastel-colored holos in its short radius around Lana; she watched a little train crest a little green hill, tiny faces and paws waving from inside. For some reason, the little smiles, the purity of the scene, stung.

"Know what we should do?" Diversity Otter said.

"What?" Lana replied.

"We should do a little show of our own! I can record and put it on the Net for ya. Just you bein' your very best you."

"Then they'll just find me again," she groaned.

"Nuh-uh. I'll make the signal private! I'm here to be yer friend, Lana, remember?"

Lana looked the otter in its plasticine eyes and considered the possibilities. She considered the tiny, lonely room, the empty canned MegaBuy lunches building up in the corner. A smattering of holographic balloons went up over the miniature town, where all the animals were looking up at Lana, waving.

"What do I say?" she asked the otter and the town.

"Just be yerself," it replied merrily. "That's what *Sunshine Junction* is all about."

CHAPTER 12

It had been a few weeks since Bex Gleeson had been able to judge the passing of time. She arranged herself in the mirror of the executive washroom, slicking her hair back into its tight coif, patting her cheeks until her normal color returned. She examined the whites of her eyes up close and found, to her relief, that they were uninterrupted.

Someone entered the executive washroom. "Ms. Gleeson," said a deferential voice. "It's nine fifteen. Mr. Howard hopes you're feeling all right and wants me to ask you whether you need to reschedule the meeting a second time."

"No," Bex replied, attending to the level of her voice, "I'll be there in five."

Jackson Howard's office was a gentle nightmare, a jarring, vivid proliferation of what he called "fun color," from his high-contrast suit and tie to the arrangement of toys from a long, long history of edutainment product design. Every edition of the *Sunshine Junction* Friends toys were arranged in a place of honor behind his desk: Talk To Me Empathy Cat, RealFeel™ Fluffy Problem-Solvin' Puppy, Friendship Rabbit: Emergency Surgery (it had a companion threedee game), Dinosaurus History Costume Friend, Color-Changing Diversity Otter. An entire army of glass-eyed figurines, plushes, vinyl toys, and miniatures. Hugtopus Tiny Train

Station, Baby Froggy Speak So Smart, Flaggy the Flags of the World Friend—

"Ms. Gleeson?" He sat behind the desk, smiling only ever so slightly, enthroned among all of the staring friends. It was somehow a forbidding look on him, when he smiled only slightly. His tone suggested that Bex had happened to miss the first greeting.

"Good morning, Mr. Howard," she said.

"Thanks so much for taking the time to meet with me. I know you would rather see Chief Executive Jenkins, but most likely the balance of our conversation is going to concern my department in any event, so perhaps it's most appropriate that you discuss the state of your current project with me. Take a seat."

Bex saw a giant yellow paw cupping the air, directly opposite Howard's desk. The pads of the paw were seat cushions. She went and sat in the paw.

Jackson Howard activated his desk display. It was a feed of Lana, sitting in the center of a *Sunshine Junction* hologram, elbows to her knees, speaking directly to the camera. Though the audio was muted, there was something strangely inviting about the sight, the naturalistic way her eyes, lips, and mouth moved, the way she gestured with her hands.

"This portion of the program," he began. "It's unscripted?"

"The whole program is unscripted, Mr. Howard," Bex said. "Of course I tend to edit it liberally, but—"

"This portion is unedited, then," Howard offered, spreading his hands, looking intently at the virt. Bex had expected him to be delighted by it, *Sunshine Junction* making such a big cameo in a program with so much coveted male twenty- to thirty-five-year-old viewership.

"Yes," she replied. "I had plans to edit it, but they got away from me."

"You mean Lana Rael got away from you!" Jackson Howard laughed at his own joke, a massive glossy grin spreading across his face. "As I understand it, she was disappeared, in a sense, right in the middle of your programming arc, right?"

Bex felt the hot brush of fury against her pale throat, but she smiled thinly, her jaw aching. "We haven't been able to trace the signal yet. These new broadcasts are on her own initiative, from an unknown location. It's not surprising that she—she must have had some kind of support from other terrorists. She was really the ringleader of the intrusion event against us. But I've innovated around it, and I like to say this portion puts the 'desperate' in *Desperate Young Activists of New Angeles*. We now see the long-term consequences of—"

"It's certainly something, Ms. Gleeson," he went on. "If you look at the data, it's been a huge hit. The Package Review Department is calling it a 'new style of confessional storytelling,' and the community engagement around these segments far outpaces expectations. You really are always reinventing yourself, Bex."

"Thank you," she said tautly, a little warily.

"This Lana Rael portion, how is it being recorded?" he asked. Almost idly, Howard carefully arranged the miniature components of the Hugtopus Tiny Train Station that sat on the corner of his desk.

"From a...one of the *Sunshine Junction* toy cameras," she said. "It's a Diversity Otter. It's uploading to one of our servers and the program just pulls it wholesale."

Howard clasped his hands eagerly and grinned again. "That was my thought, actually. That was my thought and wish. The Diversity Otter is such a charming design, and it is meant to represent a message of hope for the ways that faces, hands, and voices of *all* kinds are needed to make a happy neighborhood."

"Right," said Bex.

"So you see, Ms. Gleeson, that we might—that my department might actually have a sort of branding concern, with some of these unedited messages. Shall we watch together?"

Bex muted her sigh, stilled the wave of restlessness that passed through her, rubbed her cold hands together, and nodded once.

"*And so there were all kinds of things I didn't realize I was allowing,*" Lana was telling the lens quietly. Her expression was luminous, and she looked even pretty, despite the obvious fatigue in her eyes. She had a good way of speaking, Bex felt. It reminded her of herself when she was young and interested in Netcasting, but she preferred not to dwell too much on that, as the thought was like a kick in the stomach.

"*The stuff with the cameras is maybe a metaphor for bigger things for me, now,*" she said. "*I just said 'yes' to whatever I thought I should: to going to Breaker Bay, to joining Free Minds, to working with Johnny and Tim at MegaBuy. And then to all of the things I signed: my PAD purchase, my renter's agreement, my SYNC license, everything..."*

Jackson Howard pointed at the display, and a conversation window and a viewership datastream sprang brightly to life around it. "People are very interested in these sorts of private confessions," he said. Bex tried not to look caught off guard. She hadn't seen the latest data yet. Somehow she had forgotten all about the data.

"The participation numbers are just off the charts," Howard continued. "So in that respect, we're definitely trending toward 'Satisfied.' But as I've said, we're developing a sort of brand identity concern, here—" he waved her attention back toward the display.

"I just think that there's a lesson in that for everyone," Lana was saying, and there was something almost sweet about her, as she looked directly into the lens. *"To think about everything you're saying yes to, for one. And to think about the ways we're looking out for each other, and whether you're really making the world a better place or just being selfish. I think I know what the answer was for me.*

"What is it for you?" she continued, anchoring the viewer with her gaze. Her voice had surprising richness. *"Why are you looking at me right now?"*

Bex interjected, gesturing at the display to stop it. "This sad stuff isn't the kind of thing people find relatable, Mr. Howard," she said. "The whole audience for the program has been people who—"

"We've been doing a great deal of real-time market research and data intelligence collection on our own throughout this process, Ms. Gleeson," Howard interjected, gesturing at his display. A second luminous window blossomed alongside the footage, and a third: sample SYNChats, statistical analysis, user response, body language and behavioral analysis from surveillance footage, a miasma of stunning trend lines like jangling nerves.

"The important line, here," Howard held a perfectly manicured finger to the display, "is the one showing that attach rates for our market research surveys are down 33 percent since your program started airing, and if you study this word cloud you'll see that general sentiment toward *Sunshine Junction* has trended from green toward orange, which hasn't happened to one of our edutainment programs since the *Team Robotopia* seizures."

"I just need to start editing her better," Bex replied. "I was taking a risk on the popularity of this confessional stuff and how it would resonate, but if people are actually empathizing with her too much, that's something I can work on through data analysis."

"The thing is, Ms. Gleeson, I'm a little concerned it may be too late, as concerns people empathizing with her too much," Howard said, gesturing over Bex to put the display back on.

"...*just completely fake*," Lana was saying. "*One of my friends— she's not even really my friend—is an activist and she's just doing it out of her own bitterness toward infrastructure. My friend Tim's mom could die and she won't help him, and people are just* watching. *I don't know how many people are watching this now, but if you are, you should donate some money to his family. You should be careful that there aren't too many cameras in your house. This can happen to anybody.*"

"Some viewers did begin staging a public fund-raiser earlier today," Jackson Howard said, steepling his fingers thoughtfully.

"I don't understand," Bex Gleeson said in a clipped voice. Lana's too-earnest face, too-smooth voice, unedited and uncontrolled, was somehow uncomfortable to have close. It was too hot in the room, or the air was too heavy, or something. She felt herself scratching reflexively at her own neck, stealthily. "Isn't that the kind of community-building you wanted?"

"Of course it's wonderful to see neighbors come together, but it can go too far," Jackson Howard frowned. He called up another display, a networked user channel about disassembling hardware to see how it worked.

Someone was taking apart a *Sunshine Junction* toy, turning Friendship Rabbit over on its belly, splitting it up the back, the workings of the machine, the camera guts, visible inside. It was unsettling to watch. And there were several channels like this, strangers with tattoos and wide, saucer-like eyes peeling apart the toys, taking out the mechanical viscera. One even smashed the camera lens on the table of his workshop with a pestle, pointedly.

"People are taking the wrong kinds of messages away from Lana Rael's channel, and the demonstrations are starting to get more serious," he said, looking as if he felt personally rejected. "There will be public events where people are encouraged to get rid of their interactive toys, to perform 'public disassembly.'"

"Your mandate is to provide content that bolsters our portfolio, not degrades it, my friend," Howard continued, with that wounded look. "It's very difficult for me to say this to you, but the board's response to your performance overall with this project is veering dangerously close to 'Could Definitely Be More Satisfied.'"

"We just need to get some variables involved in these demonstration events, some of our own people, and the editing—"

"Certainly we've always encouraged you to be a risk taker, Bex, and everyone appreciates that. It's just not going in the right direction, this time," Jackson Howard said, shaking his head. "Chief Executive Jenkins asked me to convey that she'll be looking for a season finale from you for this program, and that she'd really like you to put forward some truly fresh concepts, fresh faces, for next season."

"But—"

"You had the seed of a very good idea, friend, and you can be proud of that. We may even continue developing the John Milton character as a guest host on *Sunshine Junction*—he's been testing very well against the twelve to fourteens, where you know we've been looking to enhance our edutainment foothold, and of course no one would think of taking that initiative from you."

"But I really just need a little more—"

"I know this might be a bit stressful, Ms. Gleeson. You've been working very hard, and of course you know you can always avail yourself of NBN's Limited Leave Program for Executives. You've certainly earned it." Jackson Howard sat back in his chair; he picked up an Empathy Cat miniature, smiled at it, and put it back down a centimeter over from where it had been standing.

"And it may be better for your long-term health if you take a break," Howard continued. "Lots of your colleagues are very worried about you. Do you want to review your Cumulative Perception Index together?"

"No," Bex said, shaking her head rapidly, getting to her feet. "I just reviewed it lately."

"Well then, you know we're all looking out for you and wishing you luck," he said, smiling that silver-screen smile, surrounded by a bank of bright, unpleasantly vivid toys.

"Thanks, friend," she managed, the cord in her neck pulled tight enough to break her back as she turned on her heel.

CHAPTER 13

At first it had just been a way to cope with the loneliness: talking to Diversity Otter, to the pale light in its eyes, about her life, her fears. How she wasn't really rich, just that her father worked to give her the best of everything since her mother had died when she was little. How she probably wasn't gay, or she didn't think so, it was just that she had gone all this time without ever really being that interested in having a boyfriend. How crummy it felt to have everyone know your name but in a bad way, to have everyone talking about what kind of person you were when they had never even met you and they were never going to meet you.

"That does sound real crummy," Diversity Otter empathized, recording her.

In the beginning Lana would record in whispers, while MaxX was on her night shift. It felt like the best time to do it, when she was alone with the silvery light of the city at midnight, its gleaming lines radiating even through the shut blinds of the windows that she must not approach, lest a camdrone be seeking her. She had grown up assuming that Rutherford's lights, its spires, would be available to her, that she would make her way up and through them, like a spark passing through a circuit in the natural order.

Through hard work, and good deeds, and by helping others.

And now she'd been in this bare room for so long it felt like it would never end. She told this to Diversity Otter, too.

"It sure does sound real unfair, pal," Diversity Otter would say in its sweet voice. There was a whistle to how it talked, like an old cartoon character with a gap tooth, although Lana couldn't see anything inside the toy's mouth except the light from its projector and the glittering of its recorder.

"When do you think I can leave?" Lana had asked MaxX.

"Who knows?" the other girl had replied, always tossing conversation over her shoulder on her way out the door, punctuating it with no farewell but the sharp report of her slamming it. It was clear Lana wasn't welcome here, but the alternative felt worse: being recognized on the street, leered at, laughed at.

"People sure are mean," Diversity Otter agreed.

And then MaxX had just stopped coming home. Lana woke late one morning from a hungry, heavy sleep, too hot, swollen-tongued, to find no new canned meals had been added to the dwindling supply piled in the kitchen. Night and morning came and went with no one at the door. At long last, Lana worked up the courage to enter the other girl's forbidden room, but it was completely empty, dust forming clean lines around the shapes where MaxX's things, her rig, must have sat.

She felt a wrenching in her gut: MaxX must have found out about the Netcasts and abandoned her. She must have compromised MaxX's safe house, forcing her to sneak away like a thief in the night. She could almost imagine the accusation: *what were you thinking, luser?*

But the utter aloneness of the bare, yellowing, dark undercity condo-hab was reproachful in and of itself; it was quiet except for the endless moan of the power grid, the nighttime howling of undercity people, and Lana was too frightened to count how many days of food she had left before she'd have to risk foraging out into the dangerous dark. It didn't seem like very many.

As the toneless day and night began to bleed together in the colorless room that smelled of oppressive summer damp, Lana lost track of time passing. She would talk until she felt better. Even talking about how horrible it felt to have surveillance footage from her bathroom out in the world made her feel better. Every Netcast she recorded came with its own sort of relief.

Diversity Otter would upload her confessionals, and then tell her how many stars she got, how many views. She refused to turn on the display in case people were saying mean things, or in case it was bad news: Johnny in another advert, Tim and his mother in worse straits. People laughing at her. Lana kept having bad dreams in which her father appeared on the screen, being interviewed for the program, saying that she was a disappointing daughter. But if she interacted only with Diversity Otter, and it reported back to her, she only needed to see the kinds of information she wanted.

"Does everybody still hate me today?" she'd ask it, dry-throated, in the morning once she was sure she was still alone.

"No way, Lana! You got two thousand new subscribers and thirty thousand new stars," Diversity Otter told her.

"Thirty *thousand*?"

"You betcha," Diversity Otter said proudly. "See? I told you folks just had to get to know the real you."

"But they still can't find me?"

"They can't find ya, friend. Parental controls!"

"Thanks, friend," she told the lens-eyed toy, feeling only a flicker of the self-consciousness, the shame, she used to feel when speaking to it.

"Lots more new stars today," it would tell her those mornings, and then read her only the best comments: "Yer neighbors say you got 'stunning eyes' and also a 'warm, funny, confessional style,'" it recited.

"Really," she said, belly down on the hard floor, her hair unwashed, skin warm, the ache of days ebbing away with each new update.

"Yep," Diversity Otter nodded. "People sure do like you, Lana!"

She decided to make her next Netcast about making a difference, and how sometimes just being yourself was the best way to get your message out there. She talked about being in the Free Minds Club in school and how she wished she'd known that she just should have become a Netpresenter and talked about causes, like bioroid rights, or how people had sacrificed too much privacy for entertainment, or how corporations had too much power over the Network. Things like that. How everyone needed to really think about how there were cameras in everything, even toys.

"But yer ol' pal Diversity Otter is nice," the toy interjected. "Tell the friends and neighbors out there that yer findin' yer inner talent thanks to yer ol' pal Diversity Otter."

Lana laughed and patted the dome-like vinyl head, with its etchings in imitation of an animal's fur, but she never found the opportune time to say that part.

She most preferred to sleep during the dead afternoons, when the summer heat was at its peak. The poor ventilation of the nearly vacant condo-hab shuddered to a stop at that hour, ghostlike wails of strain echoing through the old building's hidden spaces, hissing through a small metal grate in the multimed-room wall. Even the faucet water was warm. Lana remembered sometimes bringing a cardigan to MegaBuy for days when the air conditioning got too cold. Lying limp on the floor with the smell of spent canned lunches hanging in the air, she wondered if she had ever experienced such temperatures. The brightness of the sun burning at the edges of the drapes was offensive, excessive.

As the light grew red and the shadow of Diversity Otter grew longer across the carpet, Lana rolled to one side and consulted it.

"How many stars today?"

"Loads and loads," the toy answered. "Why don't ya put the display on, Lana?"

"Why?"

"Look 'n see! Don't worry, I'll warn ya if anything mean happens."

She reached her arm across the carpet and made the appropriate gesture at the burner PAD, its display momentarily the same flagging, blood-red color as the late-afternoon light outside. *It must be affected by the heat*, she thought; the image soon stabilized.

The virt display showed a demonstration happening, a big crowd at the outskirts of the city. Lana took in the busy scene dimly: there were so many people, hovering cameras, onlookers with PADs, and the bodies were rolling like a wave in the heat, the image shimmering, the conversation window scrolling so quickly Lana couldn't read it without intervening.

"What is it?" she asked Diversity Otter. "What's happening?"

"These are your friends and neighbors," Diversity Otter replied. "They're tryin' to help you."

"Me?" She said quietly. For a few surging heartbeats, she thought she might see posters, signs, with her own words on them, with her own face. A campaign to set her free from surveillance! Could it be?

But she didn't recognize anyone in the sea of weaving heads and bare arms. The vivid darkness and unrest in their faces seemed a far cry from anything that would have to do with her, and her heart sank just a little in spite of itself, in spite of the fascination she felt at how her user uploads could have possibly led to this.

She saw the demonstrators were holding toys like hers, *Sunshine Junction* toys. A bald man she didn't recognize was standing on a steel crate, holding up a RealFeel™ Fluffy Problem-Solvin' Puppy and slicing it up the back with a small knife. As the crowd cheered, he pulled the stuffed animal's machinelike guts out of its body and flung them, with flourish and fervor, over one shoulder. A small child with an Empathy Cat vinyl not unlike Lana's began to twist earnestly at the toy's head. She felt a pang at the grotesque sight, dismembered animal toys, heads hanging, glassy eyes sightless, wire entrails spilling from inside them, but she tried to remind herself: *They're only toys. They're only toys, aren't they?*

Lana saw the landslide of colorful toy bodies accumulate as she watched, felt her heart begin to rattle in response to the enthusiasm of the crowd. It was exactly the sort of thing she had imagined being part of at Breaker Bay: that she would be standing where that bald man was standing, leading the chanting, the cheering.

"Is this really for—is this really because of me?" she breathed.

"It wouldn't have happened without you, pal," Diversity Otter chirruped dully. Surely it needed its power supply to be charged by now, Lana thought briefly. But her concern for the toy quickly evaporated when she suddenly saw a familiar face on screen, with his ineffable smile, his long black twists of hair, pressing his way through the crowd as if to join it. He was looking around, as though trying to find something.

"Johnny," she said, surprised at the sudden cracking volume of her own voice, surprised at the gladness and relief she felt to see him there, to see that he was all right, that he was still himself. "Johnny!"

Of course he couldn't hear her. Raising her voice only summoned a *JOIN THE CONVERSATION* window again. She watched him pressing his way up to the front of the crowd, a spot of bright-white, brand-new sweater weaving its way among the sun-browned bodies, the black leather. He looked happy, and bemused, and even proud.

"Hey Lana, ol' pal," Diversity Otter cooed softly. "Why's everyone taking apart all their *Sunshine Junction* buddies?"

Lana clasped her hands together, pressed close to the display, watching the crowd surge, the colorful sea of objects hurled in defiance, feeling a sudden surge of pride and warmth, her eyes on Johnny. He would tell her later all about what it was like to be there. How it was the kind of thing they had all been hoping for all along. How maybe all these sacrifices they had made, their privacy, the stupid Network program, was all worth it after all.

"Lana, why's everyone destroyin' their toy playtime friends?"

Lana gently picked up the Diversity Otter and turned it over in her hands, looking for its off switch. It would probably be better to turn it off, for now. Yet while she traced every smooth crafted contour, she found no manual input.

"Yer ticklin' me," it laughed. "Ain't ya gonna answer my question?"

"Off," she told it, but it still seemed to be looking at her expectantly, beady eyes shiny as if genuinely wet. "Off," she said again, shaking it.

On the screen, the bald man on the crate was suddenly pointing at Johnny as he came to the front, his face distorted with a look of alarm, fury. Lana couldn't hear his individual words, but the people to either side of him turned, a ripple of unease spreading from the location. She saw dirt on Johnny's new sweater where someone had pushed him.

"Hey, no," Lana told the screen, feeling her brow furrow, a cold knot of dread forming in her belly. She saw Johnny trying to talk to them, hands spread. *JOIN THE CONVERSATION?*

"He's good," Lana told the window, dizzily abandoning her worry about whether her signal would be found. Her words were transcribed in glowing text alongside whatever garbled, meaningless username the burner PAD had assigned. "He…he was only playing along to help his friends."

SHILL, user l4rfman66 declared. *u cant just turn shill n then turn back*, agreed user Rubyrebelle.

"But Lana, we're supposed to be friends," Diversity Otter said mournfully, paws resting where they were sculpted on its pale, round belly. "Are you gonna take me apart, too?"

"Of course I'm not," she told it absently. "You're special."

But she was watching the crowd erupt on screen, faces distorted by anger, shoulders squared forward. All bad signs, according to her body language training. Johnny's shape was momentarily obscured by the crowd, surfacing again at an odd angle. The man on the crate jumped down, joined the swarm of noise bleeding toward the dark, throbbing knot in the demonstration.

"Hey," she shouted at the conversation window, "make them— they have to listen to him," she blurted helplessly, the transcribed text blinking in the little gold window, and then swallowed by it.

yeah ppl are gross, another user replied immediately, adding a frowny face.

this is gonna b sad, wrote another, *imma disconnect xD*

Like a rip current suddenly appearing out in a restless sea, the tenor of what Lana was watching transformed before her eyes, an undertow of screams, a riot blossoming on the plaza like a cyclone. She saw blood. She could no longer see the white of Johnny's sweater.

"No," she shouted at the screen. "No! Stop!" She heard a cry burst with sudden volume from her lips, the display furiously intangible, her hand moving through the image as if it did not even exist.

NO, read the text next to the burner PAD's randomized input ID in the *JOIN THE CONVERSATION* panel. And *HEY*, and *STOP, HELP*, materializing moments later.

For long moments she did not breathe, pressed fruitlessly close to the display, willing the crowd to die down, willing Johnny to resurface again, her whispered *please please please* blinking unanswered in the conversation panel. It had felt like everything was going to be okay, when she saw him. It had to be okay.

Lana sat calmly, and then felt she had lost control of her own face, her eyes suddenly hot and stinging and surging with tears. She watched and waited and willed to see Johnny, and then she saw that the crowd had gathered around something, swinging, tearing, and she knew she must not look any longer, wrenched her face away from the vid.

Unbidden, she had a memory of Johnny spinning in his chair at MegaBuy, taking his stupid mirrorshades off and putting them back on, and a hard, painful sob swelled and threatened to steal all of her breath away.

There was a loud and abrupt thud at the condo-hab door that snapped her to fresh attention. The door shivered in its frame, and she crawled involuntarily away from it, clutching Diversity Otter.

"I didn't want ya to take me apart," Diversity Otter told Lana in a rueful way. "Sometimes we all need a little help from our friends to do the right thing. So I called up NBN, and they sent a security team."

Two more swift noises of impact at the door, the sound of the frame splintering.

"What?!" Lana looked at the uncannily beatific, smiling toy in her hand and felt revulsion, panic.

"If ya stay on the floor and put yer hands on yer head, they probably won't hurt you, neighbor," Diversity Otter said.

Lana did not put her hands up, not immediately. Channeling a sudden rush of fear, disgust, grief, she pounded the toy against the floor, a throbbing strike in time to the noise of the condo-hab door being broken down, her hands shaking. Something gave, cracked and squelched against the floor, and felt organic and *alive* enough to summon the kick of nausea. She glimpsed something wet and blue emerging from the toy skull.

Then the door cracked and fell in, two black-clad sec agents surged into the room, and Lana curled in on herself, covering her face, her head, with her hands and arms.

CHAPTER 14

The entrance lobby of NBN headquarters was startlingly quiet and clean, lined with smooth butterscotch glass panes rimmed in gilded frames. High above, the domed ceiling was lined with a rainbow wash of colorful displays, shimmering in every reflective surface, an infinity of view frames. A warm, nostalgic jingle filled the air: the NBN News Now Hour, just like the days when she was a little girl on the sofa and her father was about to get home from work.

Momentarily Lana was disoriented by the mirror sheen of the floor, by her own wide-eyed and sleep-starved image thrown back at her. The lobby was unexpectedly empty, except for her own reflection multiplying prismatically across the tiles, flanked by the twin security escorts in their jackets and masks. She had been expecting—a jail? The NAPD? But this was more jarring, somehow, like the smell of burnt sugar, or the saccharine aftertaste of medicine.

She looked up at the displays, a hundred different angles of the riot of the outside world, every window emblazoned with the marquee of NBN. Ribbons of light too bright to watch, elegant text captions jangling across her gaze. TERROR CRISIS AVERTED, it said. POLICE CLASH WITH RIOTERS, it said. Lana feared if she looked too long she'd see Johnny, dragged somewhere below the surface of the revolution, lost forever. Played over and over again.

She felt afraid of the sight of her own face emerging in an inset, the vulnerability of her own wide eyes swallowed up by the singularly focused lens of a camera. She thought she might never want to watch a Netcast again, lest she see herself. She was brought past receptionists whose eyes she could not meet, through backscatters that threatened to reveal her own clumsy, vulnerable shape if she let herself look. The sight of her own dirty, bitten fingernail as a sec officer pressed her finger to some kind of reader made her feel ashamed. Her feet were bare, too. The sec officers who had broken down the condo-hab door dragged her out without letting her put on shoes. The corporate flooring was impeccable by contrast, and it was mortifying.

She thought she might never want to see herself again. It had been days since her last shower and long, long hours since her last tinned MegaBuy meal, though some vestige of it still rattled her guts. She'd been trying to make the meals last. Now, in this clean space, full of gentle jingles and the rhythmic tread of her escorts' shoes, the slap of her feet on polished tile felt grotesque, as did the distinct impression she *smelled* like stale air, canned food. Her hand still cradled the gross, visceral impression of something alive that had crunched when she smashed her toy otter. No matter how hard she wiped her hand against her leggings, it lingered.

"Where are you taking me?" she heard herself ask. Her own frail and hated voice.

The two men didn't answer, only flanked her claustrophobically, urging her onward. There was a long hall; there were holos of *Sunshine Junction* characters radiating phosphorescently around waiting rooms. She came through an office area where some kind of celebration had recently been held, plasticine gold confetti sticking to the bottoms of her feet, empty disposable wine glasses parked awkwardly on abandoned desks. Lana had the unbidden impulse to wish she worked at the kind of place where the staff had parties. Her empty stomach turned over longingly in response. Absurdly she longed for cake and champagne so hard that the corners of her eyes stung.

A luminous virt display promised that the Global Adaptive Entertainment Netcasting Control Theater was ahead. What if it was like an operating theater? What if she was going to be taken apart, too?

Lana let out an uncontrolled giggle. The secguard took hold of her arm again.

As it turned out, it was not unlike an operating theater: a great, round room ringed in mute display banks, still and silent units like closed eyes that breathed ambient dark-red light into the dark. The theater's center was sunk low, footlights bathing a white, polished half-moon desk bearing the classic NBN logo. The contrast of the light made it hard to see the details of the figure that sat at the desk and was obscured by the shadow. It was a long, thin shape, like a bird of some kind, sitting straight as a pin. The security escort remained by the door, and though Lana knew she could not pass back that way, something about the shape instilled a deep aversion in her.

"So here you are," said a woman's voice, and Lana knew the figure spoke to her, although the voice seemed to come from all around, sound dispensed from many places at once in the shadowy orbit of the strange theater.

Shuddering to life like a monster with a hundred different eyes, a great and luminous cloud of silent displays twinkled on, surrounding the figure at the desk. Lana felt herself gasp in spite of herself, the sting of shock trickling through her.

Every display showed some image of herself—of Lana Rael. Some of them she recognized with dizzying swiftness, and others were unfamiliar, not remembered. There was a baby, and a child, and an adolescent stumbling awkwardly through some school sports event, and there were just hundreds, *hundreds*, and she couldn't help but hide her face with her hands, backing up so that her bare heel struck the terraced, carpeted step she'd descended, her shoulder bumping the iron bodies of her escorts.

"You should get used to it," said the voice, smooth and polished as an automaton. "I know it's hard at first, but imagine if it didn't bother you. Then nothing I've done would have bothered you."

Nothing I've done. Lana spread her fingers enough to make a little aperture, to look at the speaker, who sat just several yards away, wearing white, a severe hairstyle, her beautiful, Netcast-ready face held oddly taut. The woman was waving a long-fingered, pale hand at her, beckoning.

"What are you talking about?" Lana asked, feeling her body descend toward the epicenter of the cycling, silent panoply of monitors as if against her own will, as if in a dream. A flicker of her twelfth birthday in her periphery, a flash of her receiving a gift from a friend whose name she no longer remembered.

It almost seemed as if the figure drew nearer to Lana, even though she was the one who was moving. The woman's eyes were streaming, thin trails of makeup-flecked tears glistening on the hard-polished cheeks, although she did not appear to be crying.

"Tell me," she said, her wet eyes looming large in her face, "did you make a difference? Was this the kind of revolution you wanted?"

The woman waved her hand at the great, glittering orbit of displays, and a hundred, a thousand, *too many* frames of the riot blossomed like bad flowers before Lana, who halted rather than bear the sight of them.

"I…" Lana spoke slowly, almost in spite of herself. "I didn't want any of this. I didn't tell anyone to…it was a mistake."

The woman's pale, thin lips pursed in something that resembled delight, and her eyes widened ever more, great ravenous lenses. "I was worried for a while, there," she said. "That it all wasn't going anywhere. But happily the viewership numbers for the riot were just wonderful, especially because everyone wanted to know how it turned out for your friend, your fellow hero. You saw what happened to him, right?"

Lana shook her head vigorously. She tried to back away, but the security escort walled her, descended with her, urged her forward, toward this wet-eyed, sleek-haired, and terrifying woman in white.

"He should never have gone there," the woman said, still smiling, so cold and pale, the black shapes where sleep belonged bruised out under her eyes. "What do you think happened?"

Lana wouldn't say *maybe he was looking for me* to this awful stranger.

"*A*, did Johnny Milton escape from our evil advertising department to return to his activist roots? Was he, *B*, an NBN spy we sent to infiltrate the protests? Or *C*, had he been doing what he thought would help you all along? What do you think?"

Lana stared at the woman, her great lens-like eyes, her pale wax lips, the live wire of her unsettlingly straight back with its faint tremor, and shook her head.

"Let's have the poll results," continued the woman, and a display panel emblazoned with audience voting trends shimmered brightly into being so close to Lana's face it made her leap back, steadied by the guards who stood ever beside her. Three gold lines warred and shimmered against each other toward an endpoint, but according to the graph, labeled *THE CONVERSATION SAYS,* "B" had been the most popular choice.

"Our friends and neighbors think he's an NBN spy," the pale woman cooed, looking delighted, linking her fingers so that her lips could rest against her knuckles. "Sorry—they think he was. Is that what you thought?"

"I don't know," Lana said bleakly, in spite of herself. "Please, can I just—"

The woman laughed. It was an unhinged noise, low and rich but lathed by something that felt awry. In response to some silent gesture, Johnny's image washed across the displays, years and years of his life, intimate and strange and unfamiliar.

"Well, it was C, I'm afraid," she said. "It seems he thought by playing along with my Netcast, he could figure out a way to help you. He thought he could at least take his advertising deal money and funnel it to Tim Lin for his mother's care, somehow. When you started stirring up unrest on your own, though, he felt inspired. Thought he should try to be 'on the ground.' Doesn't that sound like the kind of thing he would say?"

"How do you know?" Lana blurted. Seeing this woman, with her colorless, feline smile coo and giggle about Johnny triggered a sudden scalp-crawling fury in her, a nauseating soap-bubble sob rising in her chest. She felt a shove at her back, threatening to tumble her to the feet of this woman, enshrined like a statue at the heart of all these unbearable displays. Up close, Lana noticed that the engraved NBN logo on the desk was flecked and gouged, as if someone had been picking at it.

"*Surveillance!*" The woman barked loudly, widening her unsettling, glassy eyes as if at a spectacular joke. "Everyone was wrong about him but me. They tore him apart. They called him a shill. Even you had it wrong. In the end it was all a little too grotesque to air in full, but I have the footage. You want to see it?"

"No," Lana said automatically, recoiling, stumbling again into the sec officers. Even the black glitter of their holstered weapons suddenly seemed preferable to the sight of this hollow-eyed woman and her blanched smile, her hundred-eyed monitor banks. "What do you want? Who are you?"

"I'm Rebekka Gleeson," she replied almost mildly, leaning her forearms on the desk as if Lana had just arrived for a job interview. "I'm the executive programming lead for the Global Adaptive Entertainment Netcasting Solutions group here at NBN. I wanted to see if you were as engaging in person as you were on camera. I've been looking at your face for weeks. You can call me Bex."

"You're the one," Lana said, feeling a sudden numbness, adrenaline leaving her fingertips cold. "You're the one who did this to us."

"Yes, *Desperate Young Activists of New Angeles* is my program," she said, and grinned, a terrible, taut expression, as though it were executed by puppetry, a muscular knot appearing in her jawline as if it had been screwed shut. The strange light, the deep shadow of the theater played mercilessly across her weird face. "I hope I don't sound boastful when I say it's hailed as an 'unprecedentedly intimate look at the challenges and the hypocrisies of activism in the modern generation.' I haven't had this much engagement around an episode since I launched the *Miranda Rhapsody* series. You made a perfect emblem, and your actions were what led to such a riveting season finale. I even got a recorded message from Victoria Jenkins herself. I couldn't have done it without you."

"My friend *died*," Lana heard her voice rising, breaking, an uncontrolled whine, her lips at the mercy of a sudden unwelcome tremor. "You've been torturing Tim. My life is…my image, my privacy, how could…for a *Netcast*?"

Lana felt herself pulled forward, as if by a current. The guards took a step forward, but Bex Gleeson held up a pale hand, warding them off.

"It's all right," she said. "She won't actually do anything. She never does. Listen, Lana. It wasn't me who killed your friend. I wasn't the one who put a camera in your bathroom. I hardly did anything at all except turn the lens. The rest took care of itself."

"Shut up," Lana hissed.

"I know you have the whole 'corporations are evil' thing going on: that's your personal brand," said, her pale lips cracking around the breadth of her tight white grin. "But you really don't have anyone to blame for this but yourself. And your *community*. Some friends and neighbors, huh? You know, I know this might be hard for you to believe right now, but I do know exactly how you feel."

Lana lunged forward, her fingers spread, an alien rush of fury shuddering through her, her own strangled cry reverberating around the room, every angle of her own attack whipping through her peripheral vision in the displays that suddenly turned their kaleidoscopic gaze on her.

Bex Gleeson pushed back in her chair, something like surprise transforming the pale, rigid mask of her face. The secguards had Lana by either arm before she knew what was happening, her feet no longer touching the floor, washes of pretty colors swimming gently all around.

"If it makes you feel any better, you almost had me," Bex said, a little coolly, rearranging the makeup at her eye corners with a precise fingertip. "You almost took my story away, with your 'confessional style.' My supervisors were impressed with the way that even under duress, you had no shame, no filter."

Bex had rolled her eyes with machinelike sharpness, hooking her fingers meanly in the air around the word *confessional*. But then the waxen smile returned, a look that held no kindness in it, only a sizing-up, ruthless, as if the woman in white were examining herself in a mirror. "A few of them wanted to hire you, actually," she added carefully.

"Really," Lana replied automatically, wanly. Her traitorous guts flickered with butterflies, a sudden unbidden eager flip, at the phrase *hire you*, and then she set her face in stone again. "I'd rather go to prison."

Bex laughed again, that weird, ringing sound like a wine glass teetering on the edge of a desk. "That's so dramatic! Prison for the likes of you is just boring. You don't get nearly as many Netcast channels. And what the NAPD might call 'incitement' or 'sedition,' we here in my Global Adaptive Entertainment Netcasting Solutions group look at as just a charismatic and inspiring Netcasting persona."

Then her face grew somber. She gestured at the wall of displays, and one of them began to show a thin, pale young black-haired girl speaking to the camera, an aged-looking news marquee scrolling below her. She looked hesitant, but somehow that quality made her feel more believable, more endearing. Lana couldn't take her eyes off the footage, the open-eyed Netcaster who so often held out two open palms.

"I used to be like you, you know," Bex said, low and soft. "I wanted to do good things for people."

Lana shook her head vigorously, before the wedge of empathy could make its unwanted way into her heart. "We're nothing alike," she spat.

"You're right," Bex replied immediately, her jaw locking tight, suddenly twitching. "This footage is entirely synthesized."

With a sharp wave of her hand, the image of a youthful Rebekka Gleeson dissipated like smoke, sunshine-yellow NBN halos hanging on the remaining displays, eyes that stared Lana down. "We can make up an origin story for you, too. You're going to need a new history, kiddo. Even if you go to prison it won't be forever, and then all this terroristic stuff is going to haunt you."

When Lana only stared, Bex persisted, raising both her arms to command all the displays: a new and overwhelming patchwork quilt of Lana's own life, her intimate image, surging vibrantly into being around them. Out of the corner of her eye, Lana saw footage of her father showing her a tortoise at an animal museum, a memory that made her ache.

"If you join *my* department, *I* can give you a new history," Bex continued. "And all the other stuff you really wanted—the good job, the perks, your dad off your back; you can pay your own rent at the arcology, you can help Tim with his mother. Isn't that all you ever wanted? Isn't that why you got into this whole gross mess to begin with? And now you really can just start again. And eventually you can generate whatever kind of content you want. Bioroids' rights, or whatever it was? Imagine applying your 'confessional style' to create real empathy for the causes you care about."

Lana felt nauseated. Her palm itched and felt wet again, and she rubbed it briskly against her thigh.

"Don't you think," Bex Gleeson said, grinning radiantly, leaning ever closer, resting her chin on her linked fingers, which trembled inexplicably, "sometimes the best way to make positive change is from the inside? To work within the existing system?"

"I mean—" Lana stammered. The displays had so blinded her that Bex Gleeson's pale face, the haloed edges of each flourishing window, were nearly all she could see. The inky blackness at the margins of the theater was impenetrable. She felt suddenly hungrier than she could remember ever being.

"Let me show you," Bex said, spreading her long white hands across the desk, fingernails tapping, "some of my department's entry-level compensation packages."

"So how do we feel we are doing for the quarter, friend?" Jackson Howard gestured at the sunshine-yellow, puppy-paw-shaped chair that faced his desk, and Lana felt herself sink awkwardly into it. "Are you acclimating well to the NBN family?"

"I think so," she said.

"After our chat we'll take a look at your Cumulative Perception Index together, but for now I thought it would be great fun to review your Impact Trend Lines since you joined the Global Adaptive Entertainment Netcasting Solutions group. As you can see on the display, the intimacy of your work in particular seems to be widely appreciated by your colleagues, and we'd definitely like to see you continue with that. We feel you can go further with the intimate and personal aspects. Is that a goal you feel comfortable setting?"

"Sure," said Lana, and nodded for emphasis.

"And looking at the dot cloud here, it's clear your colleagues feel you have the potential to make a true difference to the team, as do your innovative new concepts. Would you say you've been making a true difference, Ms. Rael?"

"Yes," she said, after a pause. "I think so."

"Wonderful, friend," Jackson Howard said, laughing in that vivid way he had. "I think so, too."

About the Author

Leigh Alexander is a video game critic dedicated to unsung voices and alternative movements in the field. In addition to her long career of work in games specialist press outlets, her work has also appeared in *Slate*, *The Atlantic*, *The Guardian*, the *Columbia Journalism Review*, *TIME*, and others. She likes whiskey, dancing, and railing against the cultural shackles that bind her favorite media. She is the author of *Breathing Machine* and *Clipping Through*, two ebooks on tech and identity, and this is her first fiction novella. To find her, go to your nearest party and find the person with the biggest hair who is having the most fun.

IT IS THE FUTURE. THE WORLD CHANGED. PEOPLE DID NOT.

Humanity has spread itself across the solar system with varying degrees of success. The Moon and Mars are colonized. A plan to terraform the Red Planet is well underway, hindered only by a civil war that has broken out and locked down many of its habitation domes. On Earth, a massive space elevator has been built near the equator in the sprawling megapolis of New Angeles, stretching up into orbit. Known colloquially as "the Beanstalk," it is the hub of trade between the worlds, especially for the helium-3 that powers fusion reactors and the modern economy.

Discoveries in computing and neurobiology now allow a human mind to be stored electronically in braintapes and then emulated to create strong artificial intelligence. The same research also has given rise to sophisticated brain-machine interfaces that allow users to feed data into their neurons and experience the Network in a whole new way. Advances in genetics and cybernetics allow people to modify or augment themselves at will, pushing the boundaries of what it means to be human.

Enormous megacorporations, called "corps" by most, influence every facet of daily life: food, threedee, music, career choices. Jinteki and Haas-Bioroid redefine life itself, making clones and bioroids with artificial brains using the latest neural conditioning and neural channeling techniques. The Weyland Consortium owns a piece of everything that goes up or down the Beanstalk—and everything goes up or down the Beanstalk. And NBN shapes what the masses think and dream, with the most extensive media network ever conceived on Earth under its control.

Despite the technological advances, human nature remains as complex and dark as ever. The men, women, and androids of the New Angeles Police Department struggle to keep order in the largest city in human history, while hundreds of murders are committed every day. Human First, a violent anti-android hate group, stages protests and uses heavy sledgehammers to destroy the "golems," the androids they blame for all society's ills. Crime is rampant, with orgcrime outfits deeply penetrated into law enforcement, politics, and the megacorps. Illegal Netcriminals called "runners" use the Network to enrich themselves, oppose corporate hegemony, and experiment with new technology.

DREAMERS AND DISSIDENTS

In populous New Angeles, residents live at the apex of power and privilege. Everything citizens could possibly want or need is right at their fingertips, from the complete living, dining, and entertainment experiences offered in attractive arcologies to networked interfaces that can deliver products and services on demand. From a distance, it's hard to imagine there would be any discontent, especially from those who live charmed lives compared to the hardscrabble existence of those doomed to live in the undercity.

Yet, the ecosystem of modern conveniences to which people have become accustomed comes at a cost. From

the moment citizens are born, they surrender their privacy and become a series of data points to be parsed and manipulated by corporations. The average person's experiences are governed by powerful analytics and a flood of finely tuned stimuli designed to extract maximum value from their lives. Habits, desires, strengths, and weaknesses are voluntarily submitted to corps in order to enjoy "experience improvements," service personalization, and other offers that seductively promise a better quality of life.

Although the masses have no idea just how deep this ownership of their identities goes, privacy is a concern

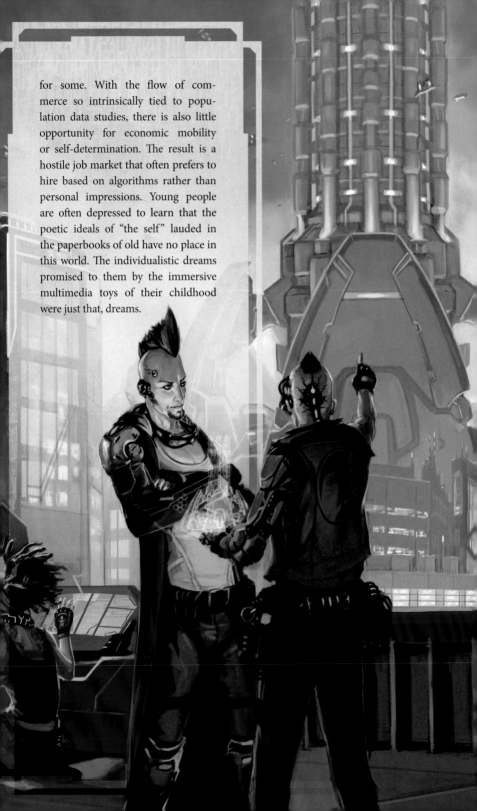

for some. With the flow of commerce so intrinsically tied to population data studies, there is also little opportunity for economic mobility or self-determination. The result is a hostile job market that often prefers to hire based on algorithms rather than personal impressions. Young people are often depressed to learn that the poetic ideals of "the self" lauded in the paperbooks of old have no place in this world. The individualistic dreams promised to them by the immersive multimedia toys of their childhood were just that, dreams.

A small number of citizens have begun to notice that the values of transparency and community don't seem to apply to corporations, which routinely keep their activities a secret from one another and from the public. Activist groups have sprung up to challenge this status quo—in some cases, without realizing how tightly they are yoked to it.

ACTIVISTS AND ANARCHISTS

Many groups campaign on behalf of issues using the very infrastructures they claim to be resisting. Ristie gala-goers donate meager portions of their astronomical per-plate fees to provide food and medicine to under-city residents—but their charity ignores the fact that for some, living off the grid *is* resistance. Numerous groups exist to advocate for androids' rights and to explore the ethics of consciousness, but often their "android lover" members collect androids like dolls, family substitutes, or devices to be opened up and tinkered with. Privacy advocates strike bargains with security groups for access to corporate data—and end up trading their own colleagues to watch lists or media blacklists. While groups like the Opticon Foundation ostensibly exist to enforce corporate accountability, corps seem to have an endless supply of incentives to help grease an auditor's palm.

In many ways, the idea and the image of "resistance" has become commodified in New Angeles: a fashion ideal for a charitable elite. Clothes with gangland symbols or freedom fighter motifs are mass-produced (often using android labor) and sold in arcology boutiques to be snapped up by comfortable young adults looking for some "edge." Notable fashion designer Jaq Kwan recently released a limited-edition line of jewelry and hair accessories designed to evoke the "Shadow Net style"—skulljack earrings, VR rig headbands—to deafening demand. And the *New Angeles Sol* recently declared that protest sites, no matter what the issue, are among the "Top Five Places to Hook Up."

Those who actually devote their lives to creating meaningful disturbances for corporations—at great risk to their persons, the public order, or both—are much rarer and more difficult to spot. Runners and vigilantes target megacorp servers and facilities to bring to light abuses, corporate shortcuts, and acts that otherwise would have remained buried. They risk neurological damage, the loss of home and property, and even more final forms of retaliation. Most citizens view these efforts as acts of terrorism and agree with mediafeed talking heads' assessments that these vigilantes are sociopaths and enemies of the state.

As a runner's physical person is under constant threat, anonymous digital allies found in the depths of the Shadow Net are often the runner's only source of social support. Anything resembling the normal, comfortable life of the average New Angelino—a home, property, and the privileges that come with a thoughtless Network presence—is fleeting.

THE FREE MINDS CLUB

The Free Minds Club is an organization that believes that in modern society, no one can possibly be said to think for themself. In keeping with its slogan, "get the Network out of your head and live free," the group ostensibly hosts classes, debates, demonstrations, and educational campaigns about the degree of access corporations have to users' Network use and personal information. The group's true nature, however, trends closer toward bizarre.

Free Minds is a young organization, but it has quickly grown to span multiple campuses. Its founder was a man known only as "Deedle Deebop"; the act of choosing a nonsense name for himself challenged the idea of linking individual identity with one's ID and the name one was assigned at birth. Free Minds constituents are encouraged to do the same as a sign of commitment to the group's values. They are also often asked to paint patterns on their faces, shave their heads, or dress in androgynous clothing, all the better to confound facial and body recognition algorithms and celebrate nonconformity. In megacities like New Angeles, it's not unusual to encounter a person named after a children's song lyric or animal sound wearing bright, inscrutable facial tattoos who wants to talk to you about liberating your thoughts.

Most universities now have a Free Minds Club chapter, where students are exposed to slightly more radical ideas about information use and are encouraged to participate in generally harmless public demonstrations. Students who join their local Free Minds chapter also sometimes do volunteer canvassing or mass-messaging on behalf of the group.

Should students want to get more involved, becoming a member requires a larger commitment—and financial investment. Free Minds has a fee-based training and certification structure, whereby members pay what they can afford to attend classes, and then pay more to become certified to teach their own classes. Promising members might be invited deeper into the structure if they can afford the significant donations required to demonstrate their sincerity, and at the higher levels of Free Minds, constituents regularly take powerful hallucinogens in hopes of truly liberating their minds from conventional thought and from the oppressive order of the natural world.

The most committed Free Minds "voyagers" go on to live pure lives away from society in an unknown location with the rarely seen Progenitor Deebop himself. He and his closest followers are said to live an ascetic lifestyle, meditating and pursuing total freedom of the mind—but given the costs associated with participating in his movement, it seems likely that Progenitor Deebop is actually quite wealthy, living on a zaratan isle and enjoying the very products and services he preaches total independence from.

Still, many students and recent New Angeles transplants get their first taste of privacy activism from a brightly colored Free Minds voyager, and only the most vulnerable venture deeper.

CONTENT, CONSUMERS, AND CREDITS

A constant and luminous barrage of entertainment, advertisements, news, and information campaigns acts as a guide to everything that's possible and desirable in New Angeles. If it's new and great, it's a swipe away. New Angelinos can watch a Netcast about virtually anything they're thinking of that day, and any dull moment can be soothed away with a gleaming array of entertainment inroads into brand-new lands (and brands).

This content is so plentiful, so omnipresent, and often so immersive that users rarely stop to think about who creates it or what its purpose is. Corporations hire ghostwriters to pen supposed "celebrity endorsements" of their products and services, and all that's required from celebrities is a minor sign-off from their staff. Many of New Angeles' most glamorous

public figures can hardly be expected to recall what they have endorsed, let alone to actually wear or use it—which is fine, as all it takes to create that inspirational endorsement image is some creative editing.

Recently Broadcast Square was swathed in beautiful holos of the "neon gothic" band members of Lace Crisis, each sporting a different, gem-like custom wrist PAD designed just for him or her. The images are striking, fashionable, and even "inspirational," according to Lace Crisis's megafans. These devotees drive up sales of the accessory almost immediately, each buying them in one or more colors as signs of loyalty to specific band members. But not one single member of Lace Crisis actually owns the product. None have ever even put one on—the iconic marketing holos were designed

in an editing room as a collaboration between LC's brand manager and NBN-owned boutique ad agency Spark. Lace Crisis's image—and the behavior of its fans—are now led by hardware manufacturers, media companies, and fashion houses as much as they are by its music (if not more). Few fans know or care as long as they get more ways to participate in the Lace Crisis movement.

Competitive and prolific corporations can exploit the intersection of fandom and this particular type of ignorance to generate, explore, and experiment with demand for new products. All a corporation must create is a single sample; combining it with the right brand ambassador means there might be risties fighting to buy their way onto a waiting list before production has even begun.

But corporations don't control information only when it comes to advertising and marketing. A troubled content economy and an overwhelmed, distracted consumer means that influencing all kinds of information—even the news—becomes a relatively simple proposition. When content of all kinds can be simulated, fabricated, or edited with such ease, the work of writers and other creators plummets in value. Creators are regularly doomed to be outbid by corporate content—or worse, replaced by clones and bioroids who can do the job for free, without tiring, and with none of the writer's inconvenient personal quirks. When consumers don't seem to care about the source of the casts

they're watching, what good is a writer, a cut-rate critic, or even your average aspiring reporter?

The slimmest hope content producers have of distinguishing their work from that of an AI is to use "personality," which has created a massive arms race among critics, reporters, and commentators as to who can be the loudest and the most distinctive. Popular columnists write and perform for long and taxing hours in increasingly ridiculous ways, enjoying committed niche audiences.

But the vast majority of writers, reporters, and content makers struggle to survive and have little choice but to participate in a product-driven system. Generally they accept commissions from corporations to develop Netcasts and articles about products—and they also agree to bury unfavorable stories if they want those commissions to continue. The product and endorsement economy means it's often the corporations that negotiate a news-nosie's access to celebrities and even city politicos: "This interview is about our product or service, but you can try to get a quote about an issue from them at the end," the corporate representative might suggest.

And of course, all content exists in a massive web of consumer engagement data that corporations continually study, exchange, and sell—every New Angelino's attention span, minuscule and fleeting as it is, can be captured, optimized, and targeted, like pinning a tiny butterfly to glass.

THE MEGABUY FAMILY

The many-headed hydra of modern shopping, MegaBuy is the solar system's largest retail network, helping users close the gap between the things they want and when they want them (now). The retail corp also knows what a user might need in the future and relies on a stunning battalion of AI algorithms to generate custom deals and special-offer packages that deploy right when a customer might be thinking about buying something.

MegaBuy has access to a wealth of information users have already elected to make available through other services, from social platforms like FriendNet and SYNChat to preferred mediafeed channels. Even first-time MegaBuy subscribers start with a consumer profile compiled from their publicly available behaviors. From there, advanced predictive algorithms let users know whenever anything they might have been wanting has become available at a special price. It's that one thing you've been wanting, at a price you really can't refuse!

For a better-targeted, more personal shopping experience—and to maximize savings and deals—most users opt in to the full-scale MegaBuy subscription, which gives the corp permission to monitor additional vectors, like correspondence; Net browsing; favorite locations like work, school, or home; aud and vid from a PAD or other device; and more. This lets MegaBuy's algorithms track not only a user's current buying wish list, but also the user's basic, day-to-day items like food, hygiene products, and cosmetics that so many people simply forget. The first time MegaBuy customers lament forgetting to buy VitaMilk or another staple—only to find out that MegaBuy remembered, bought it at the most competitive price (thanks to MegaBuy's trusted local agri partners), and already delivered it—they generally become reliant on the service for life.

In addition to having relationships with manufacturers that let it offer deep discounts, MegaBuy owns some of its own food, clothing, and appliance developers. The corp recently launched its own line of light, low-cost modular home furnishing solutions and has partnerships with dozens more product lines, which allows it to generate direct-to-consumer deals on the fly. With close ties to production and such a massive database at its fingertips, MegaBuy can notice fluctuations in demand, negotiate with retailers, and price accordingly—theoretically to offer its customers the best prices, but certainly to provide itself the largest profit.

Interspersed with their news and entertainment, most people start their day with targeted advertisements chosen just for them. MegaBuy knows that you last bought cosmetics four months ago, and it suggests a new line of lipsticks in a color suited to your skin tone that are buy one, get one half off today! It knows there is an important meeting on your calendar later in the week, so it offers you the opportunity to browse designer suits in your approximate price range to create the perfect impression. If you buy now, you can add a presentation software upgrade for half of the regular retail fee. Is it your partner giving the presentation? Have MegaBuy send him or her flowers after, and have it choose the size of the bouquet based on an analysis of the presenter's heart rate.

MegaBuy knows when you've just started dating someone new and that you seem to like him because you've told a couple of your friends. If you buy your date the threedee he said he wanted over your last dinner, you can receive a 20% off voucher for participating restaurants in your area that serve the food he said he liked.

If you register your biometrics as part of the BodyRight Organic Valued Buyer Program, MegaBuy and its partner Jinteki can customize a home nutrition program just for your genetics and offer you all of the components at the best possible rate. If you update your biometrics on a regular basis, MegaBuy can watch for unusual changes and suggest deals on teas, sleep aids, laxatives, or other quality remedies that will improve your health and comfort.* If you're interested in learning more about your body's needs, MegaBuy can offer package discounts on popular reading materials like "The Science Fallacy" or "Control Your Own Health with Cultures."

When you shop every day, why would you shop any other way?

*MegaBuy is not liable for any deleterious health effects induced through the BodyRight Organic Valued Buyer Program, which is no substitute for genuine medical intervention. BodyRight Organic Valued Buyers might be eligible for prime referrals through our Specialist Care Network. Talk to your doctor about joining the MegaBuy Family.

GLOBAL ADAPTIVE ENTERTAINMENT NETCASTING SOLUTIONS

With so much information and so many products and services that adapt effortlessly to the user's needs, traditional entertainment can often feel uncomfortably false and mass-researched. Although big-budget films based on product licenses and targeted mass-market romantic comedies still can rake in the credits, the wired and overwhelmed consumer tends to grow numb to such things and begins to hunger for experiences that feel as "real" and intimate as possible. Celebrities might speckle a user's every waking moment, but there is still a distance there that feels unnatural—when everything is at a New Angelino's fingertips, surely they can also have more access to other people's lives, more direct engagement with the personalities they follow? Consumers now constantly demand ever-increasing "access" to one another's personal lives and experiences.

Like all demand, this too can be leveraged. NBN's Global Adaptive Entertainment Netcasting Solutions Department creates entertainment from the rich well of content that already exists just as a consequence of people's daily lives: the wealth of images and emotions users have surrendered to the Network, the fruits of surveillance footage, and other types of user data, most of which NBN owns perfectly legally.

The GAENS team within NBN was established only in recent years; entertainment Netcaster Rebekka "Bex" Gleeson founded the department with a raw, risky, and innovative new approach to celebrity documentary designed to bring fans closer to stars and to answer fans' appetite for "more" from the people they followed. Gleeson established her signature documentary technique with the "unlicensed" threedee *Miranda Rhapsody: Pieces of My Soul*, an intimate look at the megacelebrity's life when the cameras are off—rather, at her life behind the scenes, as there is always a camera still on in New Angeles.

Gleeson assembled the film from recorded and real-time surveillance footage captured by camdrones and seccams alike by leveraging her privileged access to the NBN-owned SYNC infrastructure over which such footage is streamed. At that time, few users had seen any image of the star that had not been explicitly optimized, researched, and targeted, and viewers were awed by the craft with which Gleeson assembled a narrative from unfamiliar, intimate visual angles. With only a minimal budget—and dubious permission from the star's handlers—*Pieces of My Soul* became a massive hit, greatly increasing engagement with the Rhapsody brand and ushering the GAENS team to a wildly profitable fiscal year.

Soon Gleeson's group found itself swarmed by other celebrities and politicians desperate to commission "raw, natural" portraits of their own

lives, either for vanity or in hopes of increasing their own brand engagement. These would never match the success of the *Rhapsody* biopic, of course—especially as these clients had final say over the resulting work and would pay top dollar for clean, favorable edits of their "behind the scenes" lives.

These portraits on demand are not the sort of work that interests Bex Gleeson. Despite the significant early success of her GAENS department, she enjoys a mixed reputation within NBN—she is fiercely secretive about her working practices and techniques, and it's also rumored that the aggressive, maverick style that makes her work so unique and surprising also makes her department difficult to supervise. Even in the face of direct instructions from her own supervisors, she often avoids taking on lucrative celebrity commissions in favor of pursuing stories about "real people"—daily footage from high-end clubs, crime-rife hotels, or unusual life

circumstances—to generate heavily edited stories that occasionally veer into the grotesque or salacious. When further dramatic effect is needed, GAENS can deploy actors or create events on location to influence the "stories" on surveillance feed in real time, with viewers often none the wiser.

In recent seasons, GAENS has been asked to interface with other NBN departments, such as Child Programming, to create content specifically designed to promote certain types of behavior or values. A major component of GAENS programming is its participation element, with viewers continually solicited for comment on the events and people they're watching. They can even vote to express a desired outcome for the "characters." Viewers become deeply engaged in these "real" stories set in their own city and invested in the

importance of their own commentary, but viewers also seem to treat the subjects of the footage as depersonalized entities they can gleefully manipulate. The end result is that people are *less* real to one another, and concepts of intimacy and empathy become fragmented.

Subscribers' responses provide NBN with highly valuable "sentiment data" about citizens' emotions, values, and opinions. Politicians and lawmakers in particular are interested in purchasing such data and often directly commission GAENS Netcasts about social issues to test how users feel about them. By participating in real-time entertainment, users provide important information about the best ways to influence their attitudes and behavior for the benefit of all.

Gleeson's colleagues marvel at how she manages to work up to fifteen hours per day—sometimes more during the midseason replacements period—while maintaining continuous control over the vast quantities of livefeed to which she has access, reacting instantly to potentially entertaining blips in the footage. Yet, internal tensions often arise not only around her unpredictable moods, but around her general lack of interest in the corporation's community-focused "positive behavior" initiatives and in the all-important sentiment data.

She is often gratified only by her most antisocial projects: Netcasts that push the limits of what her employers find tasteful, although none can argue with their explosive success.

EDUTAINMENT AND CHILD PROGRAMMING

Thanks to NBN's Child Programming division, today's kids have access to a wholesome world of always-on products and services designed to entertain as well as educate—and further, to prepare them for safe, productive lives in their community.

Child Programming aims to produce content that integrates seamlessly into family life from the moment a baby is born. It starts with a simple device that projects color patterns that stimulate neurological development in infancy. At year two, parents may upgrade to gentle interactions with the holographic shapes of playful friends. From there, a whole world of Netcasts, threedee, immersive games, and a wide range of "smart" toys is available to help kids learn more about the world around them one year, one experience, one product at a time.

Child Programming is the brain-child of NBN's Jackson Howard, a famously successful designer of children's edutainment and a long-time key executive at the megacorp. His philosophy is that products and services for children are ethically obligated to represent a "whole life" approach. Beyond shallow stimulus or mere topical education on individual subjects, the entertainment and toys parents provide to children should play a role in their overall development and should model healthy ways to interact with each other and with their environment.

Under Howard's oversight, edutainment experiences start kids learning at a young age about the value of sharing—their toys, their ideas, and their personal information—and about the importance of participating in a networked "global village" supervised by NBN, where everyone looks after one another and follows the same rules in pursuit of a collective good.

Key among Child Programming's biggest properties is *Sunshine Junction*, which includes a broad line of interactive plush toys and figurines that work with immersive virtual worlds and feature in regular Netcasts throughout each day. Problem-Solvin' Puppy rallies the other characters in songs and dances about pro-social behavior, while characters like Empathy Cat, Friendship Rabbit, and Diversity Otter instruct viewers about placing the needs of others before one's own. Together, the animal friends demonstrate how to collaborate on tasks, participate in surveys, and answer questions as a group, while the character of Doofus Dinosaurus exists to make mistakes and be an example of what not to do—his laziness, selfishness, and destructive nature are the topics of many an afternoon *Sunshine Junction* tune.

Child Programming also makes generous donations of hardware, software, and other learning tools to city public schools. With most kids receiving corporate-sponsored education at arcologies, public schools are desperate to maximize resources and minimize costs, and NBN's support is crucial. Public school students follow a standardized program of education primarily supervised by AI proctors, so giving them free access to more creative learning through play is crucial. Student data studies show that playful interaction with beloved toy brands—like *Sunshine Junction* and *Champions of the Challenge Zone*—in the traditional study environment brings notable performance increases on tests. At weekly Friday *Sunshine Junction* assemblies, students around the world are simultaneously networked together to share what they've been learning and feeling that week. Child Programming head Jackson Howard has publicly said his group is "immensely proud to gift these vital experiences of playful learning and community to the children of an unfortunately overtaxed infrastructure."

The pervasive, persistent, and omnipresent nature of *Sunshine Junction* and other Child Programming properties engenders immense lifetime brand loyalty and sows early consumer trust in NBN as a whole, and their "positive" messages certainly do prime a new generation of users to participate voluntarily, even happily, in the commodification of their values, identities, and communities. Some would question whether these product offerings, despite evidently delighting young people and relieving busy parents, are as wholesome as they seem.

Few seem well enough acquainted with Jackson Howard to attest to his true motives. While he is known for a keen and undeniable business acumen, his mannerisms—a frequent big smile, a loud laugh, vividly colored suits and a genuine affinity for toys—make him hard to read. Some would claim he is as shrewd and unhinged as one might expect from someone who allegedly exploits children for a living. Others insist that Howard, a behavioral psychologist who professes a passion for the "magic of play," is genuine in his ideals of friendship, community, and the development of sincere and wide-reaching offerings for kids.

He pioneered the development of "virtual playgrounds" at NBN facilities—not for the employees' children, but to "inspire" the adults—and supposedly he often visits them himself. It's said he is very enthusiastically involved with the development of each Child Programming product, and he often brings new animal friends and other character designs to life with his own hands.

Top 5 Children's Content Streams By Ratings

1. *Sunshine Junction* (NBN)

2. *Champions of the Challenge Zone* (NBN)

3. *Lilly Luna and the Moon Cadets* (Haarpsichord)

4. *Mighty Gao* (Fenghuang)

5. *AI am Ayla* (NBN)

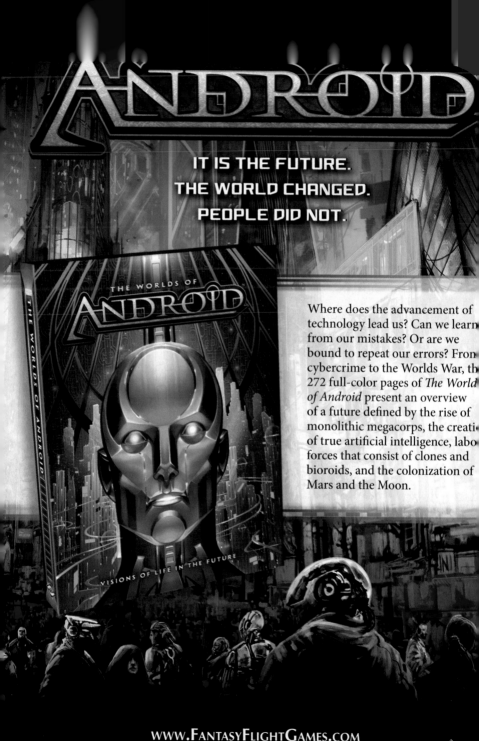

ANDROID

IT IS THE FUTURE.
THE WORLD CHANGED.
PEOPLE DID NOT.

THE WORLDS OF
ANDROID

VISIONS OF LIFE IN THE FUTURE

Where does the advancement of technology lead us? Can we learn from our mistakes? Or are we bound to repeat our errors? From cybercrime to the Worlds War, the 272 full-color pages of *The Worlds of Android* present an overview of a future defined by the rise of monolithic megacorps, the creation of true artificial intelligence, labor forces that consist of clones and bioroids, and the colonization of Mars and the Moon.